THE
CARDBOARD
KINGDOM
SNOW AND SORCERY

ALSO BY CHAD SELL

The Cardboard Kingdom

The Cardboard Kingdom: Roar of the Beast

Doodleville

Doodleville: Art Attacks!

The Stupendous Switcheroo: New Powers Every 24 Hours (with Mary Winn Heider)

THE CARDBOARD KINGDOM

SNOW AND SORCERY

ART BY

CHAD SELL

STORY BY

Chad Sell, Vid Alliger, Manuel Betancourt,
David DeMeo, Jay Fuller-Ng, Barbara Perez Marquez,
Katie Schenkel, and Jasmine Walls

ALFRED A. KNOPF NEW YORK

THE SCIENCE SQUAD
THE BUILDING BUDDIES
OWNERS OF THE DRAGON'S HEAD INN
VISITING FAMILY OVER WINTER BREAK

THE ARMY OF EVIL
THE ROGUE AND THE PRINCE BEST FRIENDS
THE CARDBOARD CRUSADERS

R OF THE
RCERESS!
THE PRINCE'S CASTLE
THE ROGUE'S DEN
CKYARD OF THE
EAST
PRINCE'S POOL
THE DRAGON'S HEAD INN
UNTER'S
LODGE
BECKY THE BLACKSMITH
BIG BANSHEE'S BOG
E GARGOYLE'S
ROOST
THE ANIMAL QUEEN'S JUNGLE
THE SCRIBE'S ARCHIVE

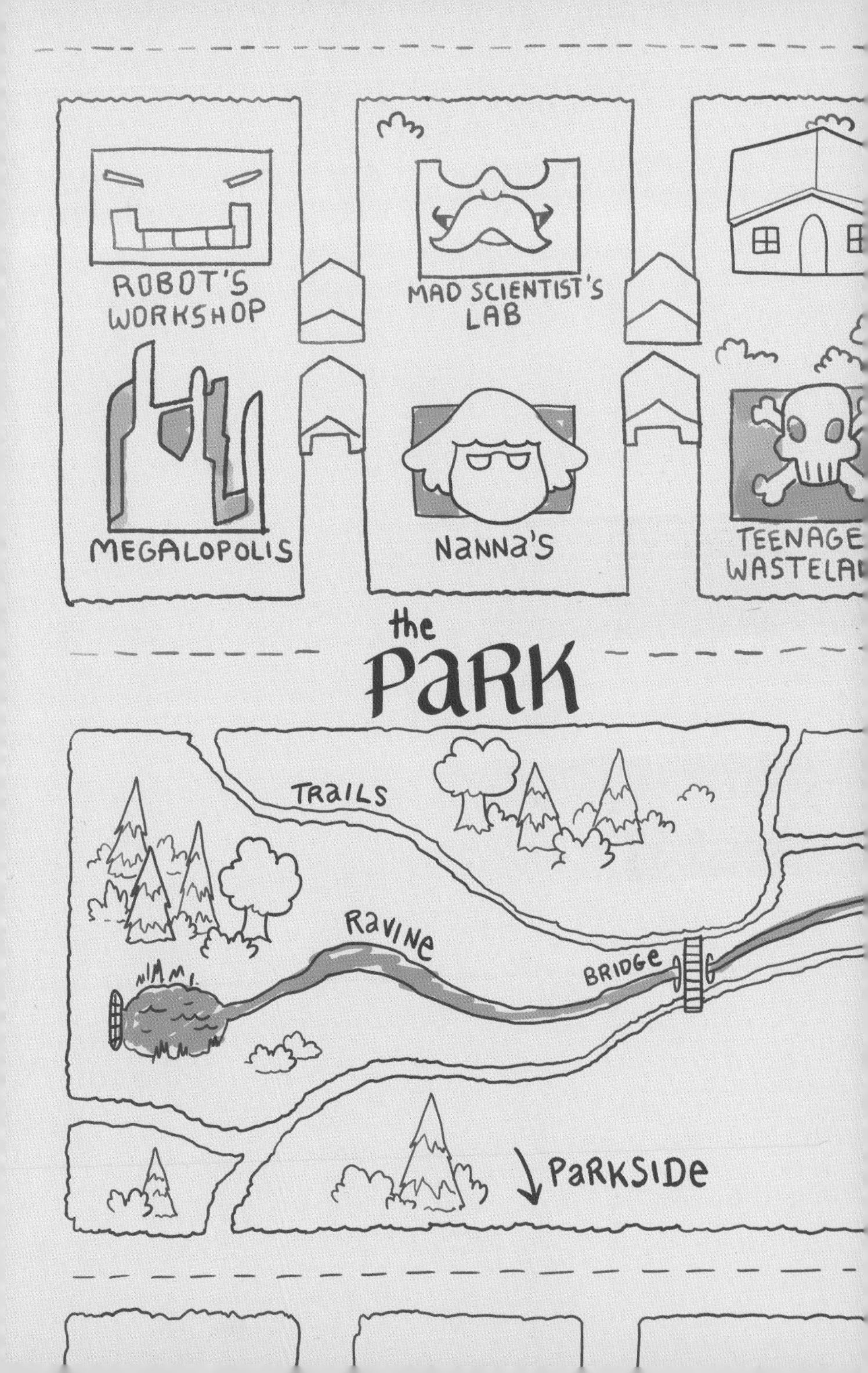
ROBOT'S WORKSHOP
MAD SCIENTIST'S LAB
MEGALOPOLIS
NaNNa'S
TEENAGE WASTELA
the PaRK
TRaILS
RaVINe
BRIDGe
PaRKSIDe

Surprise
GIFTS
and
GUESTS
WRITTEN BY KATIE SCHENKEL
ILLUSTRATED BY CHAD SELL

NO, BLUE SPARROW! LOOK OUT!
THERE'S A BOMB! AND A LASER BEAM!
WE'VE GOT TO JUMP!
AHHH!!!
KA-BOOM!!!!
I'M GLAD TO SEE YOU ENJOYING YOUR CHRISTMAS GIFTS!
PART OF ME WONDERED IF I SHOULD JUST WRAP UP SOME **CARDBOARD**.
MOM!

BUT SERIOUSLY, I DID PRETTY GOOD ON THE ACTION FIGURES?
THEY'RE SO COOL, MOM!
I CAN RE-CREATE ALL THE BIRDS OF SLAY COMICS NOW!
THANK GOODNESS RAVEN CONVINCED ME NOT TO THROW OUT MY COMICS COLLECTION!
MY EARS ARE BURNING...
RAVEN!!
HONEY, I THOUGHT YOU WERE STAYING WITH YOUR FOLKS UNTIL NEW YEAR'S!
I MISSED YOU AND SOPHIE TOO MUCH.
BUT I HAD JUST ENOUGH TIME TO FINISH MY GIFT FOR A CERTAIN SOMEONE.
IS IT ME??
IT'S YOU, SILLY.
GASP!

A BIG BANSHEE ACTION FIGURE?!
HOW?!
I WATCHED A BUNCH OF CRAFTING VIDEOS ONLINE!
YOU LIKE IT?
I LOVE IT!
THANK YOU, THANK YOU, THANK YOU!!!!
NOW BIG BANSHEE CAN FIGHT CRIME WITH THE BIRDS OF SLAY!

I ALSO SNAGGED SOME MISTLETOE!
YOU'RE A DORK.
RING RING!
OH, IT'S MY MOM.
I...SHOULD TAKE IT.
HEY, MOM.
BUT-- I THOUGHT YOU COULDN'T...
BUT...
MEEMAW?
NO, NO, WE'LL BE HERE. WE'D LOVE TO HAVE YOU.
OF COURSE. SEE YOU SOON.

APPARENTLY MY MOM IS VISITING AFTER ALL.
THAT'S A GOOD THING, RIGHT?
I JUST FEEL THROWN FOR A LOOP.
BUT HEY, NOW SHE CAN FINALLY MEET YOU!
AND IT WILL BE HER FIRST TIME MEETING BIG BANSHEE, TOO!
...RIGHT.
WELL, THAT WILL BE FUN!
I'M SURE SHE'LL BE HAPPY TO SEE YOU AND YOUR COSTUME!
IN MY DAY, GIRLS KNEW TO BEHAVE AND BE QUIET.
NOT ACT LIKE A HELLION
OR YELL LIKE A BANSHEE.
I'M... NOT SO SURE.

THE UNDERCOVER ANDROID
WRITTEN BY VID ALLIGER
ILLUSTRATED BY CHAD SELL

RUN, RUN AS FAST AS YOU CAN!
YOU CAN'T CATCH ME, I'M THE...
THE...
OH.
AHHHHH!
BEEP. BOOP.
CONNIE!!

WHY AREN'T YOU DRESSED YET?
YOUR AUNTIE AND UNCLE WILL BE HERE ANY MINUTE!
MUST DESTROY ALL DESSERTS.
THIS IS MY PRIME DIRECTIVE.
I DON'T THINK SO, YOUNG LADY!
NOT UNTIL YOU'VE DESTROYED **DINNER**!
I MEAN...
YOU KNOW WHAT I MEAN.
PLEASE DON'T DESTROY ANYTHING.
NEW DIRECTIVE: DESTROY DINNER.

HOW ABOUT YOU MARCH UPSTAIRS AND PUT ON YOUR NICE NEW DRESS?
ERROR! HUMAN DRESS IS INCOMPATIBLE WITH MY HARDWARE.
HONEY, IT FITS. TRUST ME.
TRY TAKING OFF THE ROBOT SUIT FIRST.
OOOH...
DON!
WHAT?
THOSE ARE FOR DESSERT.
OH... SORRY.
CONNIE, LISTEN TO ME.
WHEN YOUR AUNT VIVIAN GETS HERE...
I NEED YOU TO BE ON YOUR BEST BEHAVIOR.
THAT MEANS NO ROBOT STUFF, OKAY?
...DOES NOT COMPUTE.

CONNIE, TAKE OFF THAT ROBOT SUIT AND PUT ON THE DRESS!
PLEASE, FOR ONE NIGHT, JUST...
JUST TRY TO ACT NORMAL!
SWEETHEART...
I...
I DIDN'T MEAN...
DING-DONG!
OH NO, THEY'RE HERE!
CONNIE...
YOUR MOTHER, SHE'S A LITTLE STRESSED OUT RIGHT NOW.
I DON'T WANT TO WEAR THE DRESS.
I KNOW, BUT IF YOU DID, IT WOULD MEAN SO MUCH TO HER.
SHE CARES A LOT ABOUT WHAT HER SISTER THINKS.

HEY...
DID YOU KNOW THAT SOME ROBOTS LOOK AND ACT JUST LIKE HUMANS?
THEY WEAR HUMAN CLOTHES AND EVERYTHING!
YOU WOULD NEVER KNOW THAT THEY'RE MADE OF CIRCUITS AND STEEL.
HMM?
THEY'RE CALLED ANDROIDS.
SORT OF LIKE... UNDERCOVER ROBOTS!
UNDERCOVER ROBOTS?
YEAH!
INITIATING PLAN...

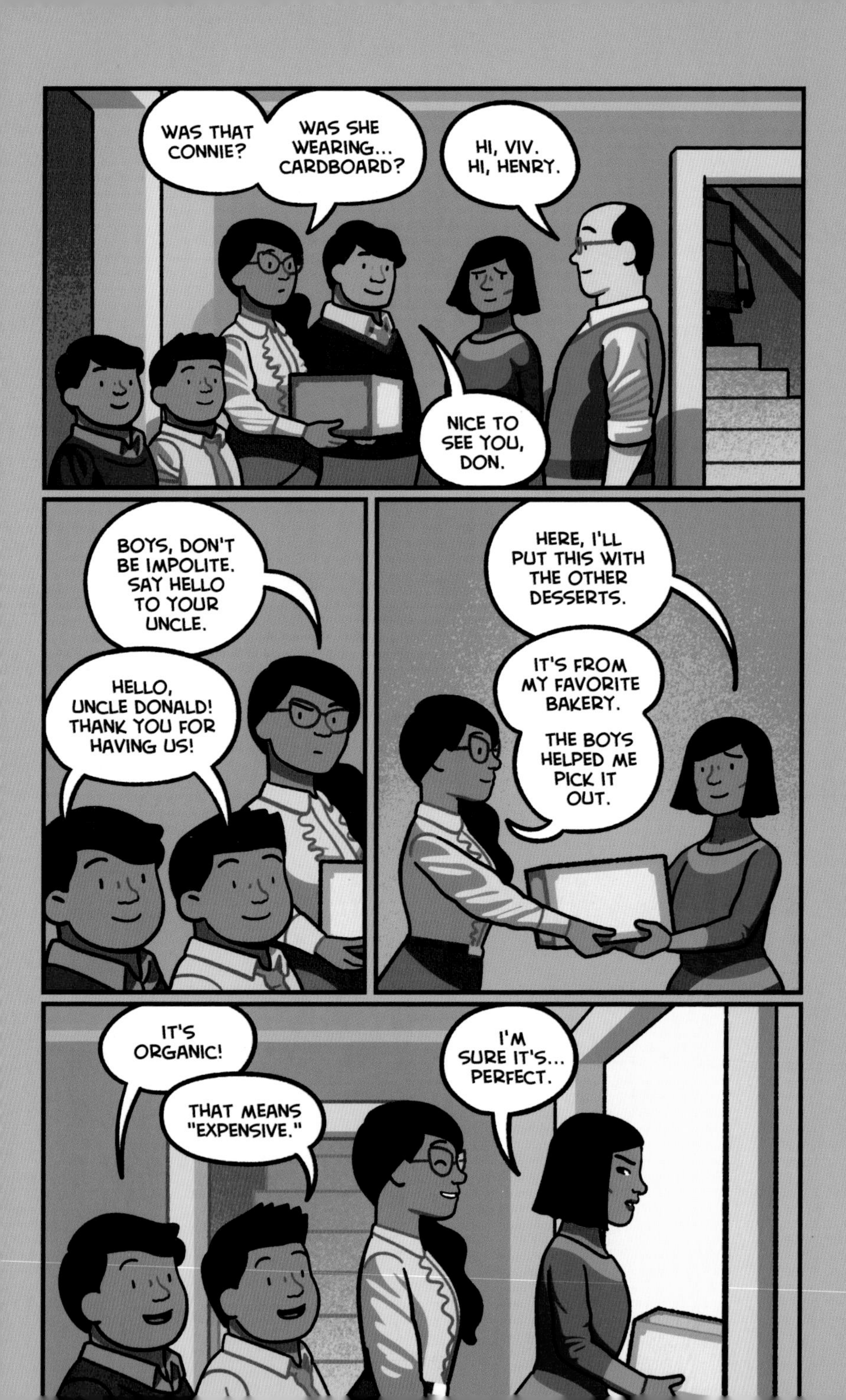
WAS THAT CONNIE?
WAS SHE WEARING... CARDBOARD?
HI, VIV. HI, HENRY.
NICE TO SEE YOU, DON.
BOYS, DON'T BE IMPOLITE. SAY HELLO TO YOUR UNCLE.
HELLO, UNCLE DONALD! THANK YOU FOR HAVING US!
HERE, I'LL PUT THIS WITH THE OTHER DESSERTS.
IT'S FROM MY FAVORITE BAKERY.
THE BOYS HELPED ME PICK IT OUT.
IT'S ORGANIC!
THAT MEANS "EXPENSIVE."
I'M SURE IT'S... PERFECT.

CONNIE!
HELLO, EVERYONE.
HEY THERE, CONNIE!
WHAT...
WHAT DID YOU SAY TO HER?

IT'S NICE TO SEE YOU, CONNIE.
IT'S NICE TO SEE YOU, TOO.
IT'S SO NICE TO SEE THINGS, ISN'T IT?
I LOVE USING MY EYEBALLS!
EVEN THOUGH THEY LACK ZOOM LENSES AND X-RAY VISION.
IS SHE... OKAY?
IT'S NICE TO SEE THAT LAMP!
IT'S NICE TO SEE THOSE CURTAINS!
IT'S NICE TO SEE THAT WALL, WHICH--AGAIN--I CANNOT SEE THROUGH.

AHEM!
LET'S GET SEATED AT THE TABLE, OKAY?
DINNER'S ALMOST READY.
DINNER!
A MEAL CONSISTING OF FOOD!
WHICH I REQUIRE TO SURVIVE!
HA HA!
PLEASE HURRY, MOTHER!
WITHOUT FOOD, I WILL PERISH!
UM, I THINK YOU'LL BE OKAY FOR A FEW MORE MINUTES.
WE FEED HER...
ALL THE TIME?

EVERYTHING IS DELICIOUS, JUDY.
THANK YOU.
YES, EXCELLENT NOURISHMENT!
I LOOK FORWARD TO DIGESTING IT!
IN MY STOMACH!
HAHAHA!
EDMUND, SIT UP STRAIGHT!
THEODORE, ELBOWS OFF THE TABLE!
YES, MOTHER!
YOU AREN'T LITTLE KIDS ANYMORE.
YOU KNOW BETTER, DON'T YOU?
YES, MOTHER.

LATER...
I HOPE EVERYONE SAVED ROOM FOR DESSERT!
OOF, I'M STUFFED!
BUT I DON'T KNOW IF ANYONE ATE AS MUCH AS CONNIE HERE.
SHE WAS A REGULAR EATING MACHINE!
...MACHINE?
THE HUMANS GROW SUSPICIOUS.
MUST LAUNCH ATTACK BEFORE DECEPTION IS DISCOVERED.

FOOLISH HUMANS!
YOU FELL RIGHT INTO MY TRAP!
OH NO...
BEHOLD MY TRUE FORM!
THE ROBOT RISES AGAIN!
UM, CONNIE...
BEEP. BOOP. YOUR DOOM IS IMMINENT!
MY WHAT IS WHAT?!

YOU ARE FIRST TO GO, COOKIE HUMAN.
BEEP!
BOOP!
DELICIOUS!
EDMUND!
THEODORE!
THAT IS ENOUGH!!

JUDY, I'M SURPRISED YOU'RE ALLOWING ALL THIS!
I MEAN, REALLY, DO YOU THINK THIS IS NORMAL BEHAVIOR FOR A GIRL HER AGE?
I...
NORMAL?
DOES NOT COMPUTE.
WHAT IS NORMAL?

JUDY?
WHAT ARE YOU DOING?!
BEEP. BOOP. HAVING FUN.
THIS IS MY PRIME DIRECTIVE.
I'LL GET THE DADBOT SUIT!
HENRY!
AREN'T YOU GOING TO DO ANYTHING?
WHAT IS YOUR COMMAND?

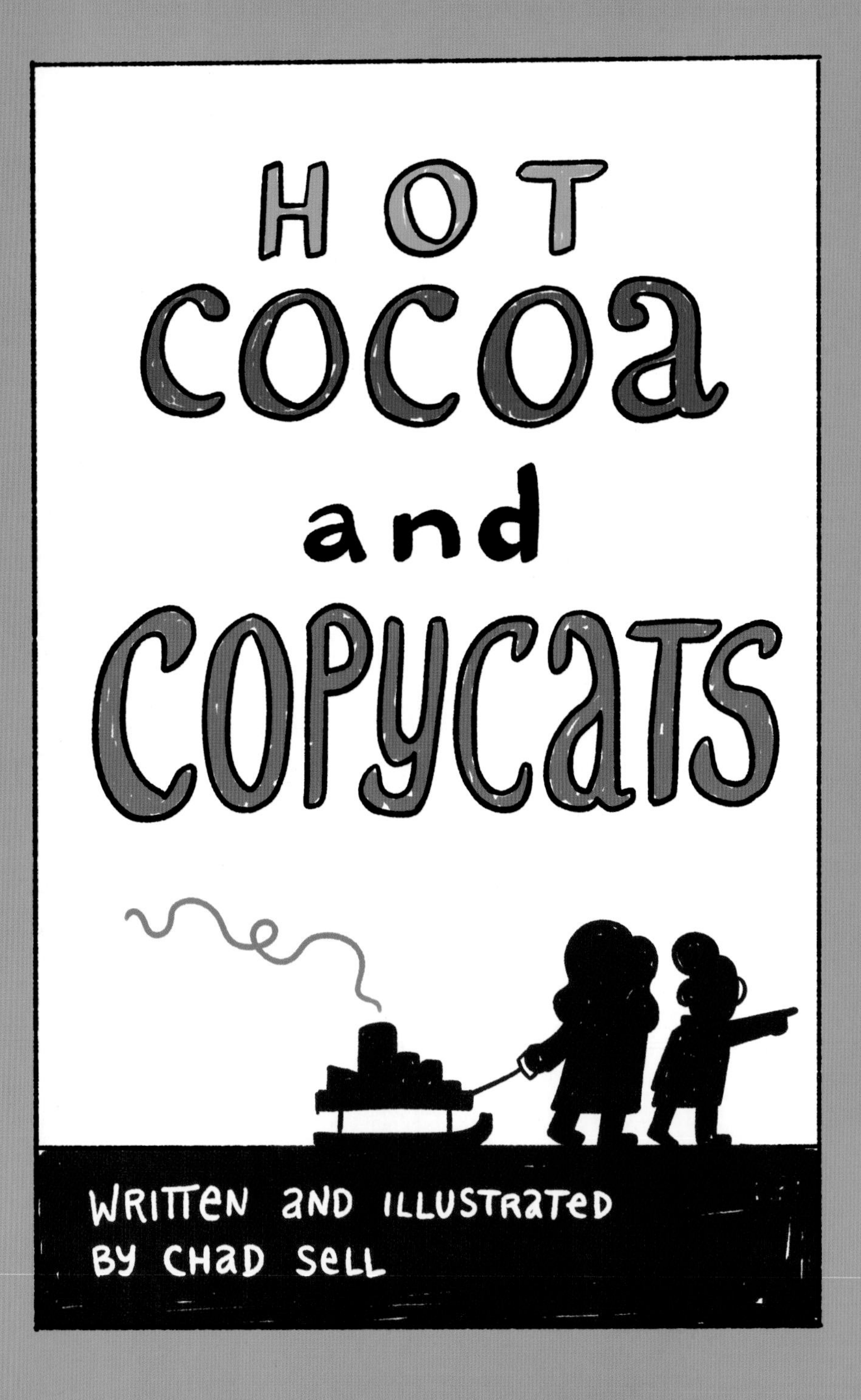
HOT
COCOA
and
COPYCATS
WRITTEN AND ILLUSTRATED
BY CHAD SELL

THE DRAGON'S HEAD INN
COCOA TOBOGGAN COMING THROUGH!
WHO WANTS SOME STEAMING HOT CHOCOLATE?
SINCE WHEN DOES THE DRAGON'S HEAD INN DO DELIVERY?
EVERYONE'S BEEN PLAYING IN THE PARK!
WE HAVE TO GO WHERE THE CUSTOMERS ARE!
DO WE?
IT'S WARM AT THE INN!
AND THERE'S A LOT LESS SNOW.
BUSINESS IS ABOUT RELATIONSHIPS, ALICE. PEOPLE SKILLS!
YOU SHOULD REALLY TRY TO WORK ON THAT.
HMPH.

WOW! A SNOWBOT!!
HI, CONNIE!
ARE THESE YOUR COUSINS?
HI! I'M BECKY.
THIS UNIT IS CALLED BEEP.
THIS UNIT IS CALLED BOOP.
GREAT, CONNIE MADE MORE ROBOTS.
JUST WHAT WE NEEDED.
SOON OUR ROBOT ARMY WILL BE COMPLETE, AND THE ANNIHILATION WILL COMMENCE!
AW, YAY!
HERE'S SOME COCOA TO FUEL THE ROBOT REVOLUTION!

PETER! ROY! THIS IS AMAZING!
IS IT THE CITY PETER MADE LAST SUMMER?
MEGALOPOLIS?
DIDN'T YOU TRY TO DESTROY IT, ROY?
I-- SURE, AT FIRST.
BUT THEN WE TEAMED UP.
ROYZILLA AND PETERTRON!
WHAT AN AMAZING TEAM YOU MAKE!
YEAH, I GUESS WE DO.
RIGHT, PETE?

HI, ELIJAH! WHAT ARE YOU WORKING ON?
I'M ALMOST DONE.
JUST A LITTLE MORE HERE...
TA-DAAAA!
YOU'RE... FINISHED?
WHAT IS IT?

COME ON, ISN'T IT OBVIOUS?
HERE, MAYBE THIS WILL HELP.
SEE? IT'S A REINDEER.
YEAH!
I CAN SORT OF SEE IT NOW.
OOOOH...
IT'S AWESOME, ELIJAH.
I LOVE IT.
YEAH, A REINDEER.
IT WAS SUPPOSED TO BE... A REINDEER.

WATCH OUT!
IT'S DANGEROUS!
GET AWAY FROM THE CREATURE!
HUH?
YOU SHOULD LET **US** HANDLE IT.

SEE ITS LUMPY FLESH?
ITS EVIL EYES?
IT'S... A ZOMBIE REINDEER!
WOW, THAT SOUNDS BAD!
I'D BETTER SLICE IT UP BEFORE IT EATS OUR NEW FRIENDS!
YEAH!
STOP!

I WON'T LET YOU WRECK ELIJAH'S EVIL REINDEER!
OH YEAH? WHO MADE YOU KING OF THE KINGDOM?
HE'S NOT THE KING, HE'S THE PRINCE!
WELL, I'M HAPPY TO HELP, YOUR HIGHNESS!
WE DON'T NEED YOUR HELP.
REALLY?
BECAUSE YOUR PRINCE WON'T PROTECT YOU!
SO IT'S A GOOD THING WE SHOWED UP FOR SOME ZOMBIE CHOPPIN'!
HEY!!
YOU CAN'T JUST COME OVER HERE AND WRECK STUFF!
WHO DO YOU THINK YOU ARE?

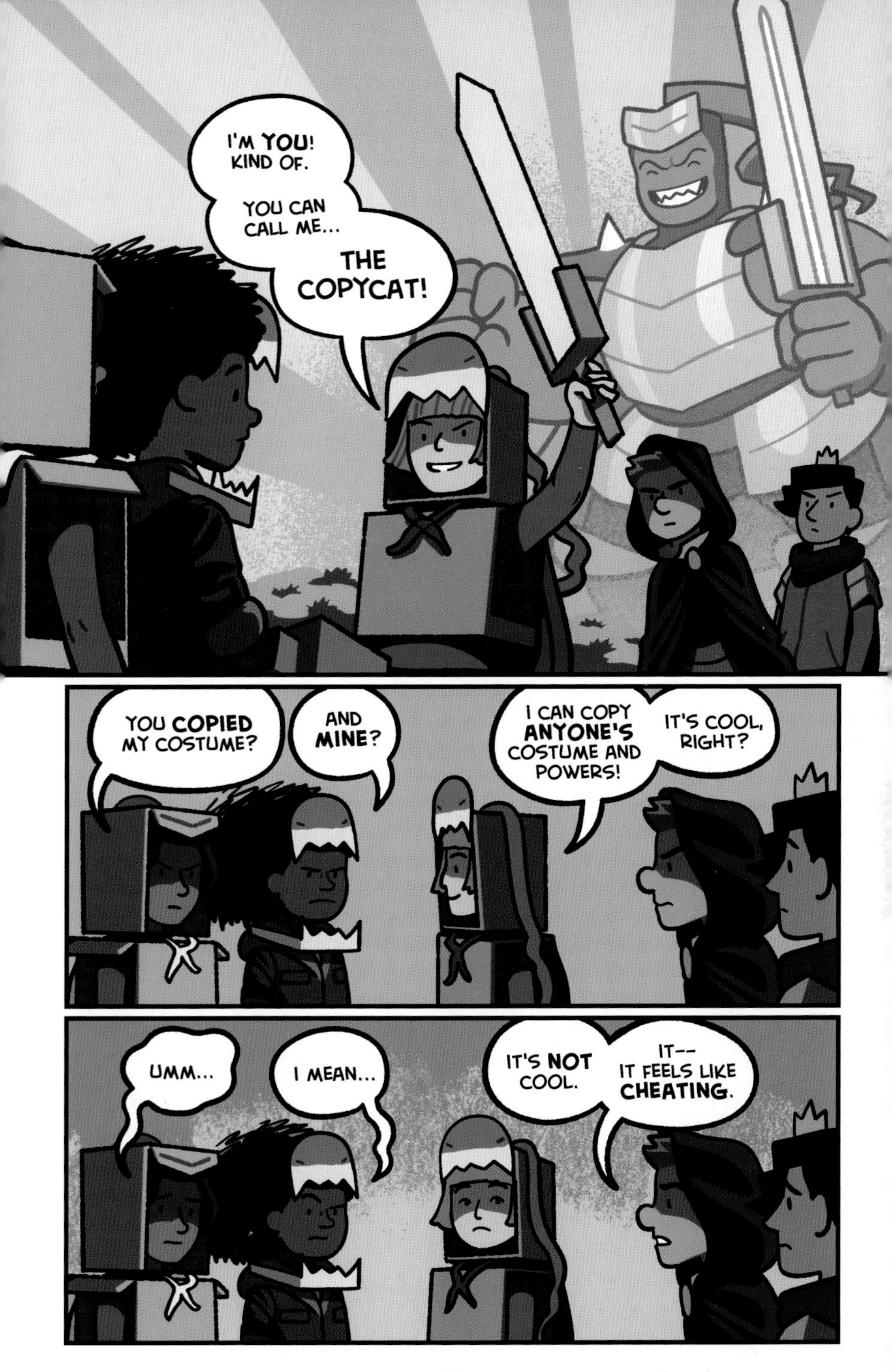
I'M YOU! KIND OF.
YOU CAN CALL ME...
THE COPYCAT!
YOU COPIED MY COSTUME?
AND MINE?
I CAN COPY ANYONE'S COSTUME AND POWERS!
IT'S COOL, RIGHT?
UMM...
I MEAN...
IT'S NOT COOL.
IT-- IT FEELS LIKE CHEATING.

HOW DO YOU KNOW SO MUCH ABOUT DARK MAGIC?
WHERE DID YOU COME FROM?
WE'VE COME FROM FARAWAY LANDS TO JOIN THE CARDBOARD KINGDOM!
FARAWAY? AS IN ACROSS THE PARK?
YOU'RE FROM PARKSIDE?
YES! AND I KNOW THE DARKEST OF MAGICS!
BECAUSE I AM THE MISTRESS OF MYSTICISM...
THE SUMMONER OF SPIRITS...
THE NECROMANCER!

WAIT, WAIT--
YOU'RE A BOY DRESSING UP AS A DARK MAGIC DIVA?!
YEAH, SO?
THAT'S MY THING!
OH?
DO YOU FEEL THREATENED BY ME?
BY YOU?
NO, OF COURSE NOT.
WELL...
MAYBE YOU SHOULD.

WHAT'S YOUR DEAL, MR. MONEYBAGS?
AHEM.
IT'S ACTUALLY MR. MILLIONAIRE.
BECAUSE I'M AN ACTUAL MILLIONAIRE.
HA! YEAH, RIGHT.
YOU DON'T BELIEVE ME?
LOOK, CAN'T YOU READ?
ONE MILLION REAL DOLLARS
ONE MILLION REAL DOLLARS

YOU MADE THAT!
YOU CAN'T JUST DRAW A MILLION DOLLARS AND--
WHO SAYS?
I CAN DO WHATEVER I WANT.
BECAUSE I'M A MILLIONAIRE.
THAT'S HOW IT WORKS.
THAT IS NOT HOW IT WORKS!
YOU'RE A COMPLETE AND UTTER FRAUD!
THERE'S NO NEED TO BE JEALOUS--
JEALOUS?!
GET OUT OF HERE!
ALL YOU PARKSIDE JOKERS, GET THE HECK OUT OF HERE!!!

DON'T WORRY...
THEY HAVEN'T SEEN THE LAST OF US!
YOU THINK I'M THREATENED BY YOUR COOL COSTUME AND EYE MAKEUP?
YOU DON'T KNOW WHO YOU'RE MESSING WITH, NECROMANCER!!!
I THINK THEY JUST WANTED TO PLAY WITH US.
EVEN IF THAT WAS AN ODD WAY TO SHOW IT.
ODD? THEY WERE CRIMINALS!
THAT WAS COUNTERFEIT CURRENCY!
THAT'S ILLEGAL!
ALICE, REMEMBER? PEOPLE SKILLS.
YOU WANT TO BE PART OF THE CARDBOARD KINGDOM, HUH?
WELL, WANNABES AREN'T WELCOME!
NEITHER ARE CROOKS!
OR COPYCATS!

A SHORT TIME LATER...
UM, SOOO...
WHO WANTS TO WARM UP AT THE DRAGON'S HEAD INN?
I ACTUALLY HAVE TO GET GOING.
MY MOM IS PICKING ME UP AT NANNA'S SOON...
AND I STILL HAVE SOME PACKING TO DO.
HIS MOM?
I THOUGHT SHE HAD... **PROBLEMS**.

WHAT DID YOU SAY?

UH, WHAT I **MEANT** WAS--
YEAH, I **KNOW** WHAT YOU MEANT.
MIND YOUR OWN BUSINESS, ALICE.
MY MOM IS **FINE**.
EVERYTHING IS FINE NOW.

TAP TAP
HA HA!
SEE YOU LATER, PETE!
I'LL SHOW YOU MY NEW PLACE SOON!

WRITTEN BY DAVID DEMEO
ILLUSTRATED BY CHAD SELL

HOW IS THE PACKING GOING, MY LITTLE PUFFIN?
PRETTY GOOD!
BUT...
WILL YOU BE OKAY HERE ON YOUR OWN, NANNA?
WHO'S GOING TO TAKE CARE OF YOU?
MY SWEET SPARROW!
YOU'LL BE RIGHT ACROSS THE PARK IF I NEED YOU.
BUT...
DON'T YOU WORRY ABOUT ME.
HONK HONK!
SHE'S HERE!

MOM!!
KIDDO!
HOW WAS WORK?
BUSY! YOU ALL READY TO GO?
SURE AM!
IF YOU NEED **ANYTHING**...
I KNOW, MA.
BYE, NANNA!
LOVE YOU!!

HERE WE ARE!
HOME SWEET HOME.
OH.
IT'S...
IT'S SO EMPTY.
THERE AREN'T EVEN ANY PICTURES ON THE WALLS.
I WAS HOPING YOU COULD HELP WITH THAT.
NANNA SAYS YOU'RE QUITE THE ARTIST!
LET'S GET YOU SETTLED, THEN WE CAN HANG OUT.
I'M THINKING JAPANESE MONSTER MOVIE MARATHON?
SOUNDS PERFECT!

I KNOW YOUR ROOM'S A LITTLE SMALL, BUT...
IT'S GREAT, MOM!
EVERYTHING'S **GREAT**!
I THOUGHT WE COULD SCOPE OUT THE NEIGHBORHOOD TOMORROW...
GET THE LAY OF THE LAND?
EXCELLENT!
OKAY!
GET SETTLED, AND I'LL QUEUE UP THE KAIJU!

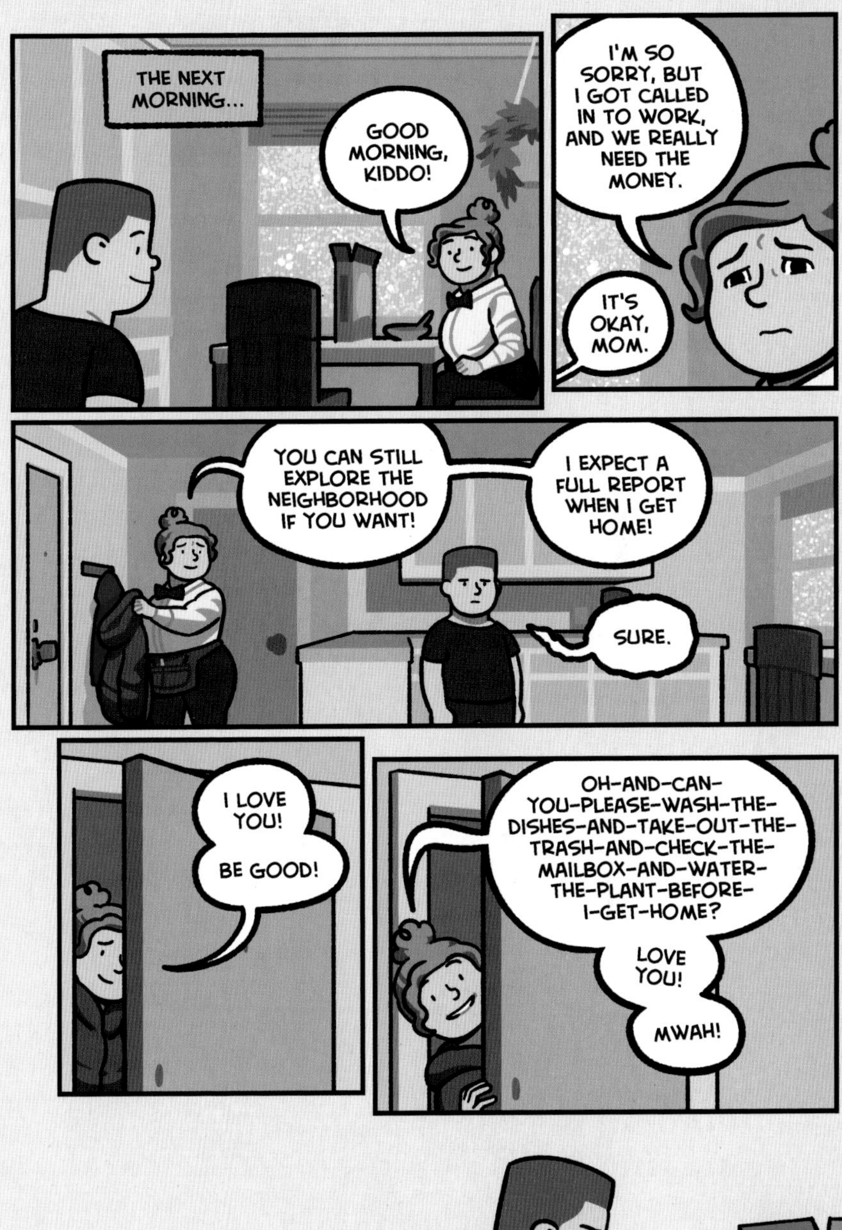
THE NEXT MORNING...
GOOD MORNING, KIDDO!
I'M SO SORRY, BUT I GOT CALLED IN TO WORK, AND WE REALLY NEED THE MONEY.
IT'S OKAY, MOM.
YOU CAN STILL EXPLORE THE NEIGHBORHOOD IF YOU WANT!
I EXPECT A FULL REPORT WHEN I GET HOME!
SURE.
I LOVE YOU!
BE GOOD!
OH-AND-CAN-YOU-PLEASE-WASH-THE-DISHES-AND-TAKE-OUT-THE-TRASH-AND-CHECK-THE-MAILBOX-AND-WATER-THE-PLANT-BEFORE-I-GET-HOME?
LOVE YOU!
MWAH!

JUST FLAKES

NIGHT FALCON
NIGHT FALCON

LIKE MOM SAID...
MIGHT AS WELL SCOPE OUT THE NEIGHBORHOOD.
NOT THESE KIDS AGAIN...
HEY.
HELLO...?
ROY.
YOU'RE THE BUILDER, RIGHT?
YOU MADE THAT LITTLE SNOW CITY IN THE PARK?
YEAH.
AND YOU WORK WITH THE QUIET KID?
ME AND MY MOM JUST MOVED IN DOWN THE STREET.
FANCY THAT.
PETER? YEAH, HE'S MY BEST FRIEND.
EVEN THOUGH YOU LIVE IN PARKSIDE NOW?
WHY WOULD THAT CHANGE ANYTHING?
MAYBE IT WILL...
MAYBE IT WON'T.
WELCOME TO THE NEIGHBORHOOD, ROY.

HEY, MOM.
HEY, PUMPKIN!
HOW WAS YOUR DAY?
IT WAS GOOD.
I DID ALL THE STUFF YOU ASKED.
I SAW! IT LOOKS GREAT IN HERE!
WHAT ARE WE DOING TOMORROW?
OH, SWEETIE, I HAVE TO WORK THE NEXT THREE DAYS.
I...
I HAVEN'T SEEN YOU IN SO LONG!
AND NOW I DON'T GET TO SPEND ANY TIME WITH YOU AT ALL!!
HONEY!
YOU'RE SEEING ME RIGHT NOW!

YOU KNOW I HAVE TO WORK.
I'M SUPPORTING THE BOTH OF US.
I KNOW.
IT STINKS.
HA HA, WHO YOU TELLING?
HA HA!
IT'S YOU AND ME, BUDDY. RIGHT?
AND NANNA.
RIGHT!
SPEAKING OF NANNA, DIDN'T YOU PROMISE TO SHOVEL HER DRIVEWAY TODAY?
OH MAN! I FORGOT!
PETER MUST ALREADY BE THERE!
DO YOU WANT A...
SLAM!!
RIDE?

I'M SORRY I'M LATE!
HAVE YOU BEEN HERE LONG?
SORRY, PETE.
OH, MY LITTLE CHERUBS...
WOULD YOU LIKE SOME SNACKS WHEN YOU'RE DONE?
YES, PLEASE!

NOW TELL ME ALL ABOUT YOUR NEW APARTMENT!
UH, WELL...
IT **ISN'T** WHAT I THOUGHT IT WOULD BE, BUT...
UH...
BUT IT'S GOOD TO BE WITH MOM AGAIN.
I MISSED HER.
YOU HAVE EVERYTHING YOU NEED?
IS YOUR ROOM BIG ENOUGH?
IS THERE ENOUGH FOOD?
GEEZ, NANNA, DON'T WORRY!
IT'S... IT'S GREAT!
EVERYTHING'S **GREAT**!

HAVE YOU HAD PETER OVER YET?
NO?
I... GUESS NOT.
WHY DON'T YOU TWO HAVE ONE OF YOUR FAMOUS SLEEPOVERS?
I'M SURE MOMMY WON'T MIND A FEW PILLOW FORTS.
OH.
UH...
YOU KNOW, THAT REMINDS ME!
WE'RE NOT, UH, FINISHED WITH MEGALOPOLIS, RIGHT?
WHY DON'T WE HEAD OVER TO THE PARK?
PLEASE?
I CAN'T DO IT WITHOUT MY BUILDING BUDDY.

HAVE FUN!
BE CAREFUL!
STAY WARM!
HA HA, WE WILL, NANNA!
CALL ME IF YOU NEED ANYTHING!

AAAAAGGGHHHHH!!!!

WRITTEN BY VID ALLIGER AND CHAD SELL
ILLUSTRATED BY CHAD SELL

MIGUEL!
I JUST HEARD.
HOW BAD IS IT?
IT'S **BAD**.
THEY GOT **ALL** OF THEM.
EVEN...?
DANG.
LET'S GO!

CONNIE! YOUR SNOWBOT IS TOTALLY SMASHED!
WE WILL NOT REST UNTIL WE GET RO-VENGE!
PETER! ROY!
ALL YOUR AMAZING WORK ON MEGALOPOLIS...
IT'S RUINED!
WE CAN ALWAYS REBUILD. RIGHT, PETE?

OH, ELIJAH...
I'M SORRY.
THAT'S OKAY.
IT...
IT WASN'T VERY GOOD ANYWAY.
HUH?
WHAT ARE YOU **TALKING** ABOUT?
OF COURSE IT WAS GOOD!
YOU DID **GREAT**!

THAT WAS THE BEST REINDEER I'VE EVER SEEN!
IT WASN'T SUPPOSED TO BE A REINDEER!
OH.
YOU DECIDED IT WAS A REINDEER.
I... I JUST WANTED TO HELP, ELI.
THAT'S HOW IT ALWAYS GOES.
I MAKE SOMETHING THAT NOBODY UNDERSTANDS...
AND YOU TRY TO HELP.
BUT WHAT'S THE POINT?
MAYBE I SHOULD SAVE EVERYONE THE TROUBLE AND STOP MAKING STUFF.

HMM...
WE MIGHT BE ABLE TO DETERMINE WHOSE BOOTS SMASHED THESE BUILDINGS.
CAN YOU SKETCH THE FOOTPRINTS FOR OUR RECORDS?
RIGHT AWAY, PROFESSOR!
SUCH SENSELESS DESTRUCTION!
WHO COULD HAVE DONE THIS?
ARE YOU SERIOUS?!
IT WAS THOSE PARKSIDE KIDS!
WE WOULDN'T WANT TO MAKE ANY ACCUSATIONS WITHOUT SUFFICIENT EVIDENCE!
EVIDENCE?
THE FOOTPRINTS GO RIGHT OVER THE BRIDGE INTO PARKSIDE!
IT'S... CERTAINLY COMPELLING, BUT...
WE WILL DESTROY THEM ALL!!!

NATE, WHAT'S THE PLAN?
WE CAN'T JUST LET THEM GET AWAY WITH THIS!
I...
I DON'T KNOW WHAT TO DO.
MAYBE WE SHOULD JUST GO **TALK** TO THEM.
I HAVE A FRIEND IN PARKSIDE-- SHE COULD HELP!
THAT SOUNDS LIKE A GOOD PLACE TO START!
YOU CAN TALK ALL YOU WANT.
THE ARMY OF EVIL WILL BE READY TO STRIKE!

HEY, ELIJAH?
YEAH?
I HEARD WHAT YOU SAID BEFORE.
BUT I DON'T THINK YOU SHOULD STOP MAKING STUFF.
I LIKED YOUR SNOW SCULPTURE.
YOU DIDN'T EVEN KNOW WHAT IT WAS SUPPOSED TO **BE**.
SO?
I STILL LIKED IT.
WHY?

I DON'T KNOW...
I GUESS IT MADE ME FEEL SOMETHING.
ALL THOSE SMOOTH CURVES AND ANGLES...
IT'S HARD TO EXPLAIN, BUT IT SORT OF LOOKED... HAPPY.
AND IT MADE ME FEEL HAPPY, TOO.
HEY, YEAH, THAT'S HOW I FELT WHEN I WAS MAKING IT!
I MEAN...
IT WAS SUPPOSED TO BE MY MOM, BUT...
HAPPINESS IS CLOSE ENOUGH!
I THINK YOU HAVE A LOT OF TALENT, ELIJAH.
I HOPE YOU KEEP USING IT.

OBSERVATIONS
THE CRIME SCENE:
- SNOW STRUCTURES
SMASHED BY UNKNOWN
ASSAILANT
-MULTIPLE SETS OF
PPING BOOT PRINT

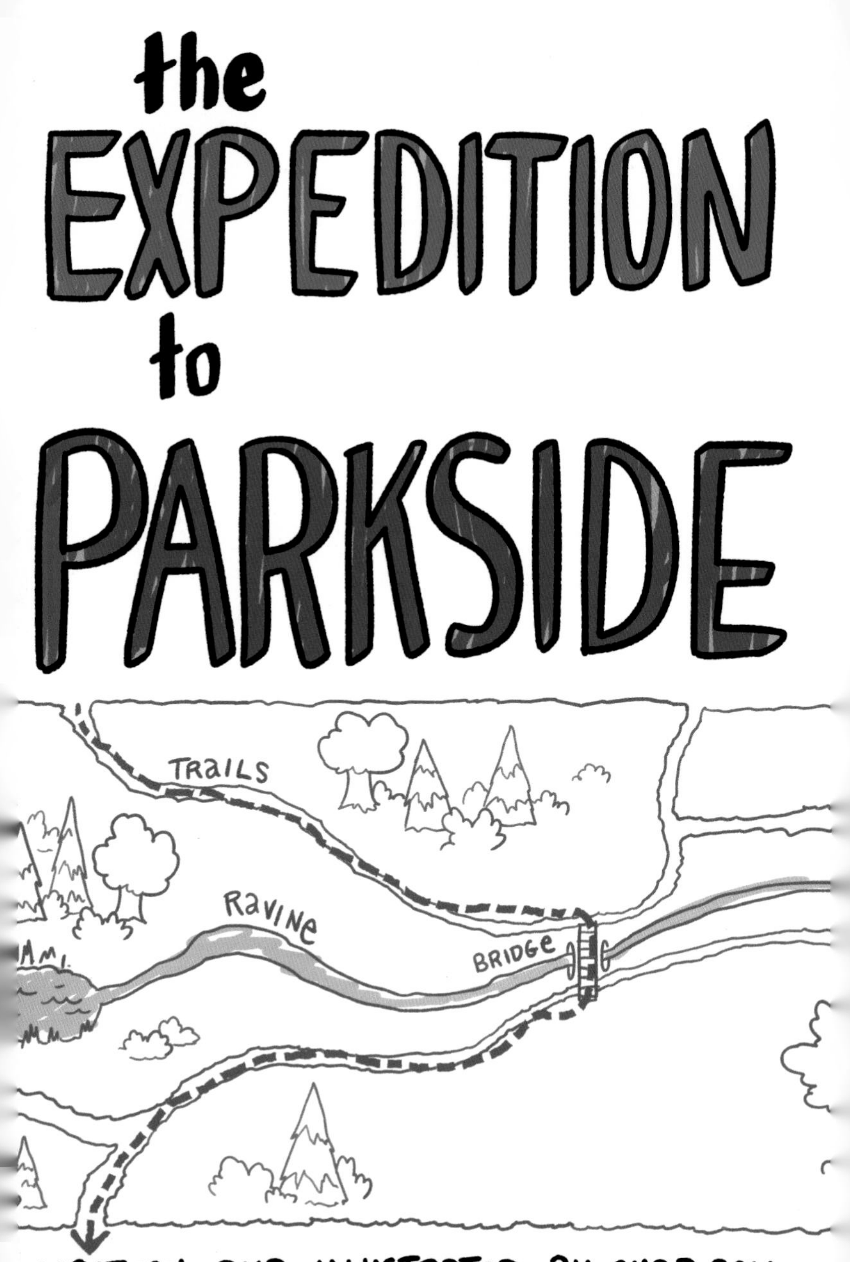

WRITTEN AND ILLUSTRATED BY CHAD SELL

WOW, SO...
THIS IS PARKSIDE?
IT LOOKS...
EXACTLY THE SAME AS OUR NEIGHBORHOOD!
NOT EXACTLY THE SAME...
LOOK, THEY APPARENTLY HAVE FLYING ROBOTS!
VMMMMMM

THEIR ROBOTS CAN FLY?!
ACTUALLY, I THINK THAT'S MY FRIEND ISABELA!
WE'RE IN ROBOTICS CLUB TOGETHER!
WHAT?
THE MAD SCIENTIST IS FRIENDS...WITH OTHER ROBOTS?!

ISABELA! HI!
OH! HI, AMANDA!
WHO ARE YOUR FRIENDS?
THESE ARE MY SCIENCE SQUAD COLLEAGUES...
THE SCRIBE AND PROFESSOR EVERYTHING.
PLEASED TO MEET YOU!
YOUR PILOTING IS INCREDIBLE!
WOW, THANK YOU!
I'M STILL FINE-TUNING MY TECHNIQUES--
I JUST GOT VALKYRIE HERE FOR CHRISTMAS.

THIS IS NO FLYING ROBOT!
IT IS A DRONE PUPPETED BY A HUMAN MASTER!
OUTRAGEOUS!
UNACCEPTABLE!
"VALKYRIE," LIKE THE FLYING WARRIORS OF NORSE LEGEND?
YES, EXACTLY!
WE CAME HERE FOR A **REASON**, SO IF YOU WOULD STOP **NERDING OUT**--
UH--
WHAT ALICE IS **TRYING** TO SAY IS THAT WE'RE LOOKING FOR THREE KIDS IN PARKSIDE.
OH?
WHAT ARE THEIR NAMES?
THE NECROMANCER.
MR. MILLIONAIRE.
AND--
AND **ME**?

FIRST YOU KICK US OUT OF YOUR KINGDOM...
AND NOW YOU COME BARGING INTO OURS?
IT'S LIKE THEY'RE OBSESSED WITH US!
WHAT?!
OBSESSED?!!
LOOK, SOMEONE FROM PARKSIDE DESTROYED OUR SNOW SCULPTURES IN THE PARK.
KNOW ANYTHING ABOUT IT?
WHY DO YOU THINK IT WAS SOMEONE FROM PARKSIDE?
BECAUSE THE FOOTPRINTS LED US STRAIGHT BACK HERE!
STRAIGHT BACK HERE?
REALLY?
MAYBE WE CAN TRACK THEM DOWN TOGETHER!

YOU'RE A SUSPECT!
WE'RE NOT GOING TO WORK WITH YOU!
CAN WE SEE IF HER BOOTS MATCH THE FOOTPRINTS?
THEN WE CAN--
WHAT?
ISABELA?
ARE YOU ON THEIR SIDE?!
HUH?
WHY DOES ANYONE HAVE TO PICK A SIDE?
WE'RE NOT AT WAR WITH EACH OTHER!
NOT YET.
LOOK, THERE'S NO NEED TO FIGHT!
NOT IF YOU SURRENDER IMMEDIATELY, PUNY HUMANS!
OKAY, I THINK WE'RE DONE HERE. BUT...THIS ISN'T OVER.
OH, I HOPE NOT!
BYE FOR NOW!

THE DRAGON'S HEAD INN

WRITTEN BY VID ALLIGER AND CHAD SELL
ILLUSTRATED BY CHAD SELL

ISABELA, CAN YOU GET THE NEWSPAPER?
SURE, MOM!
OOF, IT'S **SO COLD**!!
HMM...
THIS IS A GREAT CHANCE TO TEST OUT VALKYRIE'S CARRYING CAPACITY!
VMMMMMMMMMM
VMMMMMMMMMMMMMMMMMMMMMMMMMMM

LET'S SEE IF THIS WORKS...
PERFECT!
vvmmmmmmmm
NOW IT SHOULD BE EASY ENOUGH TO BRING IT BACK AND...
PAF!
WHAT?!

VRRKKKTTCHH!
VALKYRIE!!
PAF!
FWUMP!
WHAT?!
WHO--
MWAHAHA!!!
THE ROBOT?!

LATER THAT MORNING...
WE JUST HEARD!
WHAT HAPPENED?
ISABELA IS STILL ASSESSING THE DAMAGE.
I HOPE SHE CAN FIX IT.
THAT **DETECTIVE** IS INTERROGATING CONNIE AND HER COUSINS ABOUT WHAT HAPPENED.
INTERROGATING? DID THEY HAVE SOMETHING TO DO WITH IT?
THAT'S WHAT **ISABELA** SAYS.

ISABELA! VALKYRIE!
ARE YOU OKAY! IS IT OKAY?
CAN YOU FIX IT?
I THINK SO, BUT I DON'T HAVE THE RIGHT TOOLS.
I'VE GOT PLENTY AT MY LAB!
I'M HAPPY TO HELP HOWEVER I CAN!
THANKS, AMANDA!
THE ROTOR'S LOOSE, BUT IT SHOULD BE EASY TO FIX AT YOUR LAB.
IT'S REALLY NOT A BIG DEAL.
OF COURSE IT'S A BIG DEAL!
HUGE!
UGH.

ISABELA, THEY RUINED YOUR LITTLE ROBOT FRIEND!
IT'S NOT RUINED. IT SHOULD BE EASY TO--
DON'T COVER FOR THEM. THEY'RE NOT YOUR FRIENDS.
BUT AMANDA IS MY FRIEND.
YES, WE WOULD ALL LIKE TO BE FRIENDS!
AFTER EVERYTHING THEY'VE DONE--
THE ACCUSATIONS! THE SABOTAGE!
YOU TALK OF FRIENDSHIP?!
HEY, LET'S TRY TO CALM DOWN, OKAY?
YOU'RE THE ONE WHO STARTED THIS!
MARCHING INTO PARKSIDE LIKE YOU OWN THE PLACE!
THAT'S NOT--
LOOK, WHY DON'T WE JUST WAIT AND SEE WHAT CONNIE HAS TO SAY?

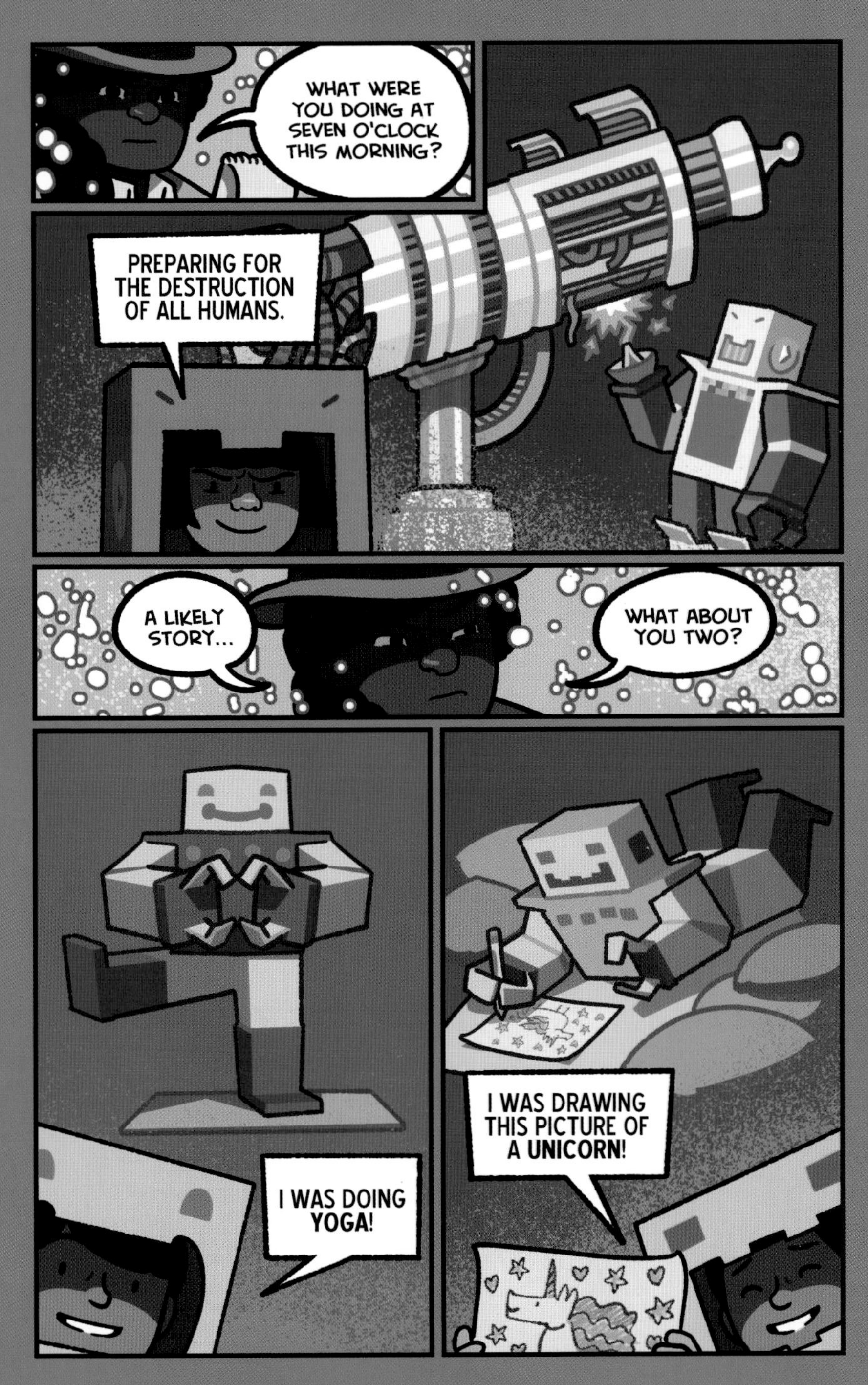
WHAT WERE YOU DOING AT SEVEN O'CLOCK THIS MORNING?
PREPARING FOR THE DESTRUCTION OF ALL HUMANS.
A LIKELY STORY...
WHAT ABOUT YOU TWO?
I WAS DOING YOGA!
I WAS DRAWING THIS PICTURE OF A UNICORN!

THE UNICORN... WILL ALSO PLAY A PART IN THE DESTRUCTION.
SO WILL THE YOGA!!
YOU SEEM AWFULLY INTERESTED IN DESTRUCTION...
THAT'S BECAUSE DESTRUCTION IS AWESOME!
ROBOTS LOVE DESTROYING THINGS!
AND IS THAT WHY YOU TRIED TO DESTROY...
YOUR FELLOW ROBOT?!
THAT IS NO ROBOT.
IT IS A PUPPET-- A TOOL OF THE HUMANS THAT DESERVED TO BE DESTROYED.
OKAY.
I THINK I'VE GOT ALL I NEED.

SEE? SHE CONFESSED!
UH, DID SHE?
THAT'S JUST HOW SHE IS.
LIKE, ALL THE TIME.
HEY, I'M MIGUEL!
I WAS HOPING YOU COULD HELP US INVESTIGATE WHAT'S--
SORRY, I WORK ALONE.
BUT...
I DON'T LIKE ANY OF THIS, MIGUEL.
ME NEITHER.
BUT...
BUT YOU'LL FIGURE OUT HOW TO FIX IT, RIGHT?
ME?
I SEEM TO MAKE THINGS WORSE EVERY TIME I SHOW UP IN PARKSIDE.
WELL, WE HAVE TO DO SOMETHING.
BEFORE IT'S TOO LATE.

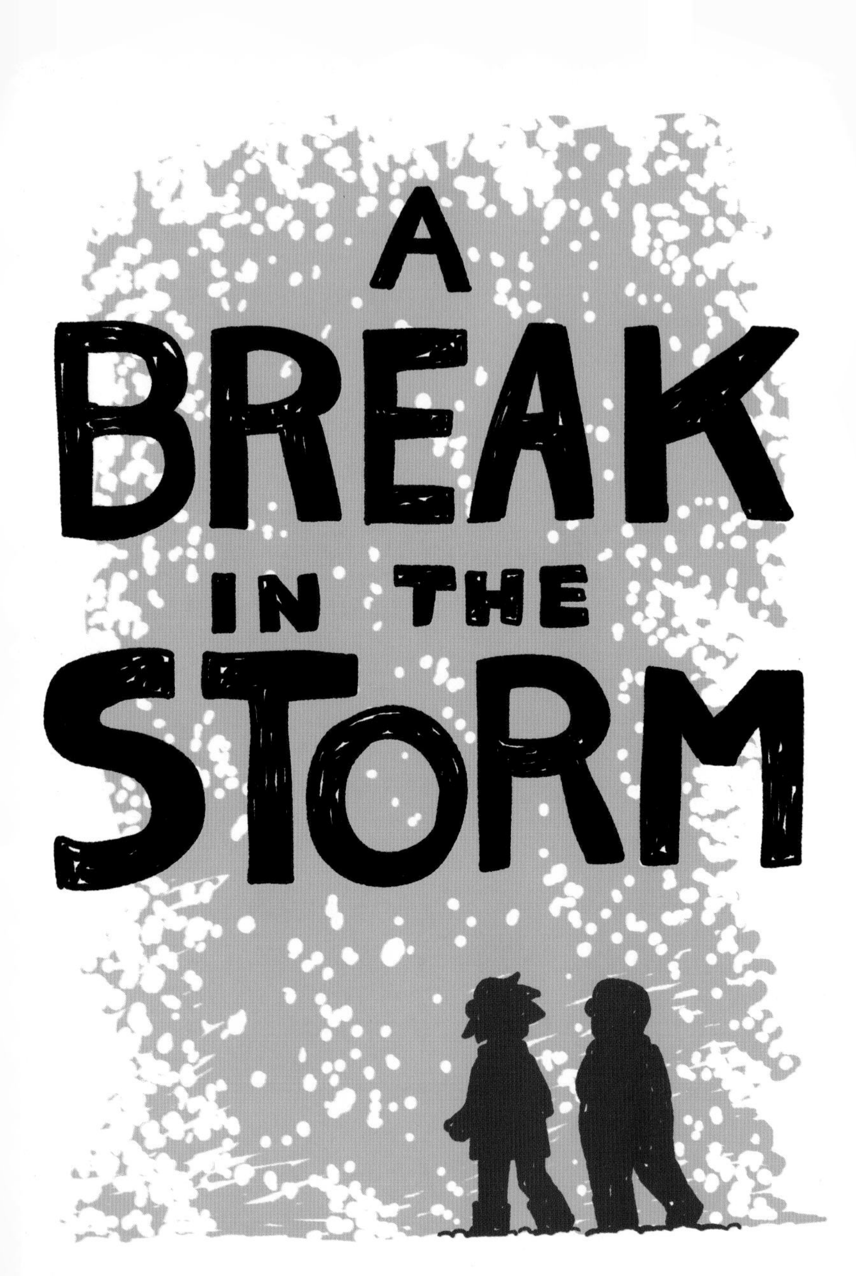

WRITTEN BY BARBARA PEREZ MARQUEZ
ILLUSTRATED BY CHAD SELL

ARE YOU SURE THIS WILL BE OKAY?
BEEP BEEP BEEP
OF COURSE!
THIS IS THE SAFEST FACILITY IN THE KINGDOM!
WHATEVER YOU NEED, MY LABORATORY IS YOURS!

AFTER SEVERAL CALIBRATIONS AND ADJUSTMENTS...
¿POR QUÉ HACE TANTO FRÍO AQUÍ?
AMANDA, WHAT DID WE SAY ABOUT LEAVING THE SLIDING DOOR OPEN--
OH! HELLO, ISABELA!
HOLA, MRS. ROJAS! SORRY FOR COMING BY UNANNOUNCED.
IT'S NO PROBLEM. WHAT HAPPENED TO YOUR MACHINE FRIEND?
VALKYRIE WAS ATTACKED THIS MORNING!
ATTACKED? BY WHO?!
BY ROBOTS!
WELL, BEFORE SKYNET TAKES OVER...
LET'S MAKE SURE ISABELA'S MOM KNOWS SHE'S HERE, OKAY?
IT'S GETTING DARK.

YOU KNOW, WE COULD MAKE SURE VALKYRIE IS READY NEXT TIME!
WHAT DO YOU MEAN?
I'M THINKING WEATHERPROOF SHIELDS...
EARLY-DETECTION SENSORS...
THAT WAY, VALKYRIE IS PROTECTED!
THIS WOULD ACTUALLY BE A GREAT PROJECT FOR THE SCIENCE SQUAD!
I'M NOT IN THE SCIENCE SQUAD, THOUGH.
WELL, CONSIDER YOURSELF INVITED!
THINK ABOUT IT: THE GREATEST MINDS OF BOTH KINGDOMS WORKING TOGETHER!
IT WOULD BE THE BEST THING SINCE...
THE INTERNATIONAL SCIENCE COUNCIL!

I DON'T KNOW...
WHAT WOULD THE OTHER CARDBOARD KINGDOM KIDS SAY?
WOULD THEY THINK I'M A **SPY**?
STEALING THE SCIENCE SQUAD'S TECHNOLOGICAL SECRETS FOR PARKSIDE?
NO WAY! YOU'D BE AN EXCELLENT ADDITION!
YOU SHOULD ATTEND OUR NEXT MEETING!
ISABELA, YOUR MOM WILL BE HERE SOON.
AND LET'S WAIT FOR HER WITHOUT RUNNING UP THE HEATING BILL, OKAY?
OKAY, MOM!
YOU GIRLS WANT TO HELP ME WITH DINNER?
I'M MAKING ARROZ CON POLLO!
YUM!

DID YOU FIX YOUR FRIEND, ISABELA?
YES, THANK YOU FOR HAVING ME, MRS. ROJAS.
IT WAS REALLY HELPFUL.
I TOLD HER SHE SHOULD JOIN THE SCIENCE SQUAD!
WE COULD USE HER EXPERTISE!
THAT SOUNDS LIKE A MARVELOUS IDEA!
THE MORE FRIENDS, THE BETTER!
IT DOESN'T MATTER THAT SHE'S FROM PARKSIDE, RIGHT?
ISABELA IS WORRIED THE OTHER KIDS WILL THINK SHE'S A SPY!
NONSENSE! IF ANYTHING, YOU ALWAYS BENEFIT FROM OUTSIDE PERSPECTIVES.
WHAT DO YOU MEAN, MRS. ROJAS?
WELL, WHEN AMANDA'S DAD AND I FIRST MOVED TO THIS COUNTRY...
WE THOUGHT WE WOULDN'T FIT IN...
THAT WE WERE TOO DIFFERENT.

BUT WE LOVED OUR NEW NEIGHBORS, AND THEY LOVED US.
ESPECIALLY WHEN I BROUGHT OVER MY FLAN!
IT SHOULDN'T MATTER WHO YOU ARE OR WHERE YOU'RE FROM.
LOOK AT THE CARDBOARD KINGDOM! YOU ALREADY HAVE HEROES AND VILLAINS AND...ROBOTS?
YOU'VE ALL LEARNED TO GET ALONG, AND YOU'RE BETTER FOR IT.
AND WE HAVE AMAZING ADVENTURES TOGETHER!
RIGHT! AND SO... WHY CAN'T THE KINGDOM GET A LITTLE BIGGER?
JUST LIKE IN THE ARROZ CON POLLO, EVERY INGREDIENT BRINGS SOMETHING TO THE MIX.
TASTY AND PRODUCTIVE!

SO, I'LL SEE YOU AT THE SCIENCE SQUAD'S NEXT MEETING?
YOU BET!

SECRET LAIRS AND SNEAK ATTACKS
WRITTEN AND ILLUSTRATED BY CHAD SELL

IN THE TOP-SECRET HEADQUARTERS OF THE ARMY OF EVIL...
OKAY, TEAM, WE NEED TO BE READY FOR ANYTHING.
THOSE PARKSIDE KIDS WILL WANT PAYBACK FOR WHAT CONNIE DID TO THEIR DORKY LITTLE DRONE.
INCORRECT. I DID NOTHING TO THE DRONE.
HUH?
WHAT?!
YOU... DIDN'T?

I THOUGHT...
DIDN'T YOU SAY THAT THE DRONE DESERVED TO BE DESTROYED?
IT DID.
BUT NO ROBOT WAS RESPONSIBLE FOR THAT.
RIIIIIIGHT!
OF COURSE! NONE OF YOU HAD ANYTHING TO DO WITH IT.
WINK!
EVEN THOUGH THE PARKSIDE KIDS TOTALLY DESERVED IT!
YEAH!
OUR STORY WILL BE THAT YOU THREW ABSOLUTELY NO SNOWBALLS AT THE DRONE.
WINK!

ARE YOUR EYES MALFUNCTIONING?
AND YOUR EARS, TOO?
I KEEP TELLING YOU! I DID NOT ATTACK THE DRONE!!!
I DIDN'T, EITHER!
NONE OF US DID!
GOOD, YOU HAVE TO KEEP YOUR STORIES STRAIGHT, NO MATTER WHAT.
DON'T ADMIT ANYTHING TO ANYBODY.
ADMIT WHAT?!
RIGHT! EXACTLY!
WINK!
HUMANS ARE SO CONFUSING.

OKAY, SO BACK TO PARKSIDE.
WE HAVE TO KEEP AN EYE ON ALL OF THEM, ESPECIALLY THE NECROMANCER.
YEAH, I BET SHE'S PLANNING SOME REALLY DARK, EVIL STUFF.
SURE, BUT I MEAN...SHE'S OBVIOUSLY JUST A CHEAP COPY OF ME, RIGHT?
I THINK HER COSTUME'S COOL!
AND HER MAKEUP IS NEAT!
BUT NO, THAT'S NOT THE POINT!
WE NEED TO BE READY!
AT ANY MOMENT, THE PARKSIDE KIDS COULD SURPRISE US WITH A--
SNEAK ATTACK!!!

THIS IS FOR VALKYRIE!
BUT I DIDN'T--
WE REALLY DIDN'T--
AND THIS IS FOR LYING ABOUT IT!
THIS IS FOR CALLING ME A **CHEAP COPY**!
WHAT, YOU HEARD THAT?!
WE HEARD **ENOUGH**!!

ADMIT IT, WE TOTALLY GOT YOU!
WE ADMIT NOTHING!!
I THINK OUR BUSINESS HERE IS FINISHED.
AW, ALREADY?
YEAH, THEY'D HAVE TO BE PRETTY BOLD TO COME BACK TO PARKSIDE.
IS EVERYONE OKAY?
NO!
NO, OF COURSE NOT!!

THIS ISN'T OVER!
YOU HEAR?!
THIS MEANS WAR!!!

the PRINCE'S PLAN
WRITTEN BY MANUEL BETANCOURT
ILLUSTRATED BY CHAD SELL

WAIT, SO...
JACK DECLARED WAR ON ALL OF PARKSIDE?
I MEAN, YEAH, BUT...
HE CAN'T ACTUALLY DO THAT, RIGHT?
NATE, I DON'T WANT THINGS GETTING OUT OF HAND.
ME NEITHER!
KIDS COULD GET HURT!
I KNOW!!
BUT EVERYONE'S EXPECTING ME TO LEAD THE CHARGE...
MAKE ALL THE DECISIONS...
FIGURE OUT HOW TO FIX EVERYTHING, BUT I DON'T--
I...I--
HEY, HEY, HEY.
RELAX, KIDDO.
COME HERE.

IT'S THIS CROWN.
SOMETIMES I FEEL LIKE I **NEVER** SHOULD HAVE PUT IT ON.
EVERYONE LOOKS AT ME LIKE I KNOW WHAT I'M DOING.
BUT IT'S JUST A PIECE OF **CARDBOARD**.
BUT YOU LOOK SO DANG CHARMING IN IT!
DAD!
YOU KNOW WHAT I MEAN.
YOUR BROTHER HAS BEEN LOOKING UP TO YOU SINCE LONG BEFORE YOU WERE "THE PRINCE."
AND THAT'S GOT **NOTHING** TO DO WITH THE **CROWN**.
THANKS, DAD.

ARE YOU OKAY, JACK?
I HEARD THEY REALLY GOT YOU!
BUT WE'LL GET THEM BACK WAY WORSE!
YEAH!
BUT THAT WILL ONLY CONTINUE THIS TERRIBLE CYCLE OF VIOLENCE!
WHO ASKED Y-- WAIT, YOU?!
IS THAT THE GIRL FROM PARKSIDE?
WHAT'S SHE DOING HERE?
HI AGAIN!
I'M... LA MECÁNICA!
THE NEWEST MEMBER OF THE SCIENCE SQUAD!

WHAT ARE YOU HERE TO DO, HUMAN?
MAKE US ALL YOUR PUPPETS?
NO, I'M HERE TO HELP FIX THINGS!
CAN YOU FIX ME, PLEASE?
I HAVE A LOOSE BUTTON.
WHAT ABOUT UPGRADES?
CAN YOU HELP WITH THOSE?
SURE! I'D LOVE TO!
WAIT! NO!
YOU CAN'T--
THE MEETING'S GONNA START!
BUT...
BUT WHAT KIND OF UPGRADES?!

AT THE MEETING...
WE NEED TO SHOW PARKSIDE WHAT IT MEANS TO MESS WITH US!
NO!
AGGRESSION IS NOT THE ANSWER!
LOOK--
RAWRR!!
LET'S SHOVE THEIR FACES IN THE SNOW!
EYE FOR AN EYE!
WE MUST USE DIPLOMACY, NOT FORCE!
WE'VE GOTTA BE READY!
WE CAN'T LET THIS GET OUT OF CONTROL!
INITIATING TOTAL ANNIHILATION SEQUENCE IN 5...4...3...2...
CAN'T WE JUST TALK TO THEM?!
EVERYONE, STOP!
PLEASE, LET'S TRY TO CALM DOWN.
CALM DOWN AND DO WHAT, NATE?
I... UH...

DON'T WE NEED TO KEEP OUR KINGDOM SAFE?
I...YES! BUT THAT DOESN'T MEAN DECLARING WAR ON ALL OF PARKSIDE!
YEAH, IT'S LIKE THAT'S EXACTLY WHAT THEY WANT.
WE NEED MORE INTEL.
MAYBE I CAN FIGURE OUT WHAT'S REALLY GOING ON THERE.
WHAT, BY SPYING ON THEM?!
YEAH!
LOOK, THIS ISN'T...
WE HAVE TO COME TO AN AGREEMENT ON--
BUT WE CAN'T AGREE ON A SINGLE THING!
HUH.
MAYBE... THAT'S IT.

YOU'RE RIGHT. WE'RE NOT GOING TO AGREE ON ANY ONE PLAN.
BUT MAYBE WE DON'T HAVE TO!
IF WE PLAN THIS WELL, WE'LL BE READY FOR ANYTHING!
SCIENCE SQUAD, YOU CAN TRAVEL TO PARKSIDE AND NEGOTIATE A CEASE-FIRE.
WE'LL TRY OUR BEST!
AND WE'LL NEED WARRIORS WATCHING OUT FOR ANY MORE ATTACKS ON THE KINGDOM.
THE CARDBOARD CRUSADERS CAN DO IT!
PETER, ROY...
CAN YOU BUILD A FORTRESS WE CAN DEFEND IN THE PARK?
SOUNDS FUN!
ALICE AND BECKY...
CAN YOU MAKE SURE WE'RE STOCKED UP WITH EVERYTHING WE'LL NEED?
C'MON, BECKY-- INVENTORY TIME!

WHAT ABOUT US?
WOULD THE ARMY OF EVIL ACTUALLY FOLLOW ANY ORDERS I GIVE YOU?
EH, PROBABLY NOT.
HEH HEH!
DIDN'T THINK SO.
JUST, UM, DON'T GET CARRIED AWAY?
REBOOTING TOTAL ANNIHILATION SEQUENCE IN 5...4...3...
MWAHAHA!

THAT WENT GREAT!
I TOLD YOU NOT TO WORRY.
BUT, MIGUEL, WHY DO YOU WANT TO GO **SPY** ON PARKSIDE?
BECAUSE THERE'S SOMETHING WE'RE NOT **SEEING** HERE.
NOT YET.
I THINK WE'RE ALL GETTING **PLAYED**.
I KNOW HOW YOU FEEL, MIGUEL.
BUT THERE'S **NOT** ALWAYS A MONSTER LURKING AROUND EVERY CORNER.
SOMETIMES A SHADOW IS JUST A SHADOW.
I UNDERSTAND.
BUT I NEED TO GET TO THE BOTTOM OF THIS.
JUST... BE SAFE, OKAY?
ALWAYS!

LATER THAT DAY...
THIS CAN NEVER HAPPEN AGAIN!
AMBUSHED IN OUR OWN HIDEOUT!
HUMILIATED BY THE NECROMANCER AND HER GOONS!
SO...WHAT'S YOUR PLAN, JACK?
HOW DO WE STRIKE BACK AT PARKSIDE?
AWAITING INSTRUCTIONS.
YOU'RE GOING TO ENGINEER THE WEAPONS OF OUR REVENGE.
HUH?
I WANT YOU TO COME UP WITH THE GROSSEST AND STINKIEST STUFF YOU CAN IMAGINE!
COOL! LIKE... A SECRET WEAPONS LAB!
EXACTLY!

WE NEED STUFF SO TERRIBLE THAT WE'D GET IN TROUBLE IF ANYONE EVER FOUND OUT!
BUT WE ARE NOT PERMITTED TO GET INTO TROUBLE.
NO EXCEPTIONS.
WHICH IS WHY NOBODY CAN KNOW WHAT YOU'RE DOING.
I DON'T EVEN WANT TO KNOW.
WE HAVE TO TAKE PARKSIDE COMPLETELY BY SURPRISE!
MWAHAHA! THIS IS GONNA BE FUN!!
NO, SAM! THIS IS SERIOUS!
...DEADLY SERIOUS.

UNLEASHING the BANSHEE

WRITTEN BY KATIE SCHENKEL
ILLUSTRATED BY CHAD SELL

SOPHIE, IS EVERYTHING OKAY?
YEAH, YOU SEEM OFF.
OH, IT'S JUST...
UH...
MY MEEMAW IS VISITING THIS WEEK.
AND I'M NOT SURE I CAN BE THE BIG BANSHEE WHILE SHE'S HERE.
WHAT?!
YOUR GRANDMA DOESN'T LIKE THE BIG BANSHEE?
SHE...
SHE HASN'T EVER SEEN MY COSTUME.
DURING HER LAST VISIT, SHE MADE SUCH A BIG DEAL ABOUT GIRLS BEING QUIET AND BEHAVED...
IT WAS EASIER NOT TO SHOW HER.
AND YOU DON'T WANT TO SHOW HER NOW?
I...
I DON'T KNOW.

I JUST WANT THIS WEEK TO GO WELL.
FOR MOM AND RAVEN'S SAKE.
I CAN HOLD BACK THE BANSHEE FOR A FEW DAYS.
OKAY, BUT DON'T HOLD HER BACK FROM US!
YEAH, THE KINGDOM NEEDS YOU!
HA HA!
I'D NEVER LET DOWN MY FELLOW CARDBOARD CRUSADERS!
OR THE KINGDOM!
BESIDES, I--
WHAT?!
OH NO!
SHE'S HERE EARLY!!

UH...
HERE, CAN YOU KEEP MY COSTUME SAFE?
JUST FOR A FEW DAYS?
THEN I'LL BE BACK TO FULL BIG BANSHEE.
OKAY, SOPHIE...
IF YOU THINK THAT'S BEST.
THANKS, CRUSADERS!

H-HI, MEEMAW.
HAPPY AFTER-CHRISTMAS.
SOPHIE!
HAPPY HOLIDAYS, DEAR!
CAN YOU HELP MEEMAW WITH HER THINGS?
THE TRIP WAS EXHAUSTING.
BUT I'M SO HAPPY WE'LL BE TOGETHER FOR NEW YEAR'S.
YEAH...
ME TOO.

THAT NIGHT...
AND THEN I HELPED HER UPSTAIRS SO SHE COULD NAP.
SOUNDS LIKE THINGS ARE GOING OKAY, THEN?
I GUESS SO...
BUT I DON'T GET IT!
I THOUGHT MEEMAW WOULD BE MAD AT ME LIKE SHE WAS LAST SUMMER.
BUT SHE'S ACTING LIKE SHE DOESN'T EVEN REMEMBER YELLING AT ME.
HMM.
YOU KNOW, SOMETIMES GROWN-UPS ONLY REMEMBER WHAT THEY **WANT** TO REMEMBER.
HUH?
THEY PRETEND SO HARD THEY DID NOTHING WRONG, THEY FORGET IT HAPPENED AT ALL.
THAT'S SO CONFUSING.
YEP, IT IS.
I'M BACK WITH DESSERT!
OUR HERO!

AHEM.
OH, MOM!
HOW WAS YOUR NAP?
FINE, DEAR.
SO, THIS IS RAVEN.
REMEMBER I TOLD YOU ABOUT HER?
SO YOU DID.
HELLO, MA'AM.
I'M SO HAPPY TO FINALLY MEET YOU.
RAVEN AND I MADE PLANTAIN CURRY FOR DINNER!
IT'S MY OWN RECIPE.
HMM, HOW **ECLECTIC**.
OKAY, SOPHIE...
OPERATION GREAT DINNER IS A GO.

...AND SHE WAS LAUGHING SO HARD AT MY JOKE...
SHE TRIPPED AND SPILLED PAINT ALL OVER HERSELF!
TALK ABOUT A BAD FIRST DAY!
WELL, I MET YOU, SO IT WASN'T THAT BAD.
SO, WHAT'S NEW IN THE CARDBOARD KINGDOM, SOPH?
OH, WELL, UH...
THE CARDBOARD WHAT?
IT'S JUST THIS THING I DO WITH MY FRIENDS.
IMAGINARY STUFF. NO BIG DEAL.
WELL, I THINK IT'S A BIG DEAL!
I CAN'T BELIEVE YOU MADE THAT COSTUME ALL BY YOURSELF!
SOPHIE, WHY DON'T YOU SHOW MEEMAW THE ACTION FIGURE RAVEN MADE?
RAVEN DID SUCH A GOOD JOB, MOM.
IT LOOKS JUST LIKE SOPHIE'S DRAWINGS OF HER MONSTER.
SOPHIE HAS A MONSTER?
CAN I SHOW HER LATER?
I'M STILL EATING CURRY!
YUM!

SO, RAVEN, YOU MAKE... TOYS?
ISN'T THAT A LITTLE...
CHILDISH?
I THINK IT'S OKAY TO BE A CHILD AT HEART.
PLUS, MY NEPHEWS LOVE MY GIFTS...
AND SO DOES SOPHIE.
Y-YEAH!
MY NEW ACTION FIGURE IS REALLY COOL, MEEMAW!
IT'S MY FAVORITE CHRISTMAS GIFT!
WELL, I'M SURPRISED YOU DIDN'T MAKE A MORE APPROPRIATE GIFT FOR A GIRL LIKE SOPHIE.
MOM...
OR PERHAPS YOU THINK GIRLS SHOULD BEHAVE LIKE HELLIONS.
WAS THAT HOW YOU WERE RAISED, RAVEN?
MOM.
UH, WOULD YOU LIKE MORE CURRY, MEEMAW?
NO THANK YOU. I THINK I'M READY FOR BED.

GOOD NIGHT, SOPHIE.
LOOK, MAYBE SHE'S JUST GRUMPY FROM TRAVELING.
WE'LL TRY AGAIN TOMORROW.
I'VE GOT A KNACK FOR WINNING OVER PEOPLE.
MOM?
ARE YOU OKAY?
EVERYTHING IS FINE, SWEETHEART.
LET'S GET READY FOR BED.

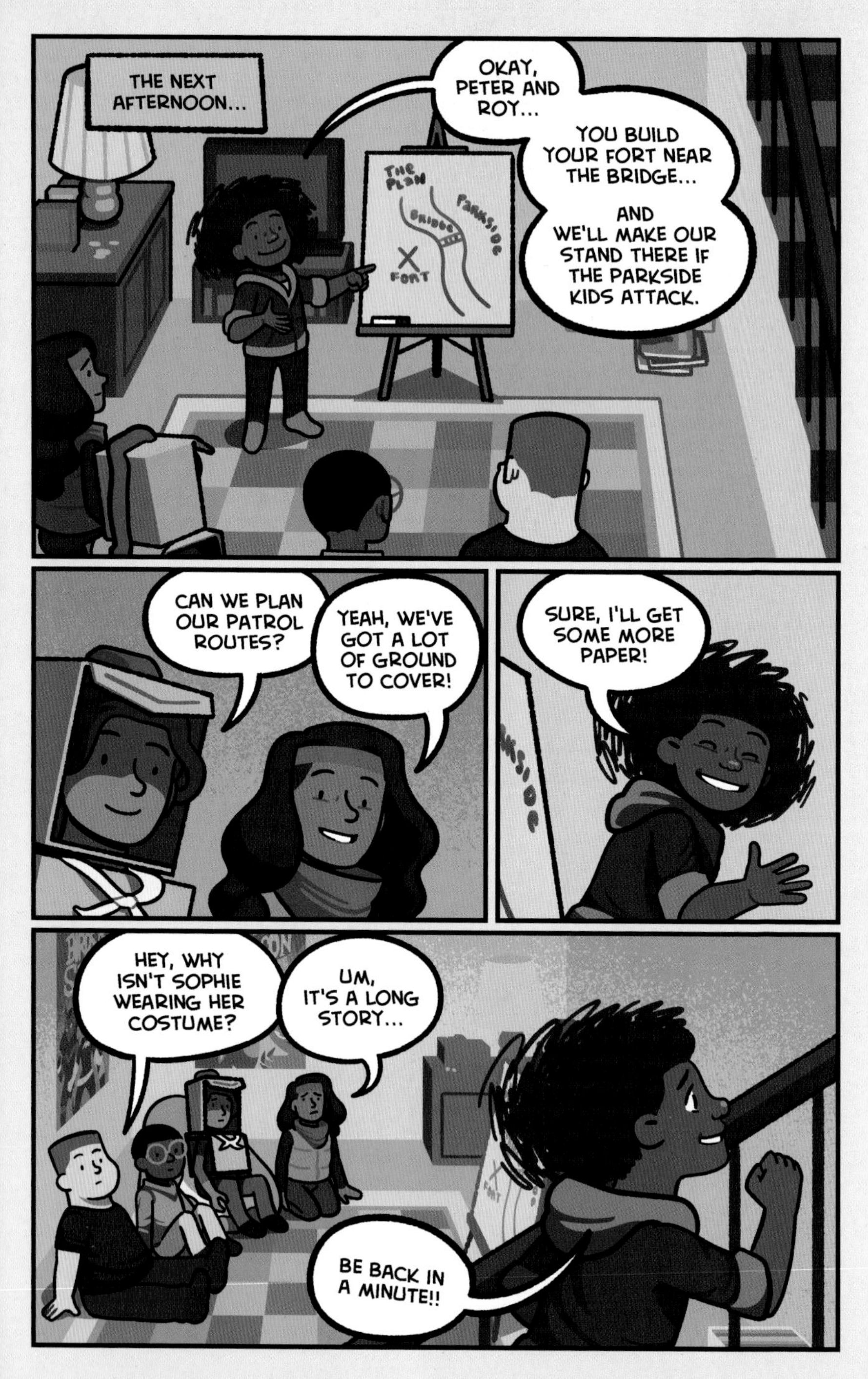
THE NEXT AFTERNOON...
OKAY, PETER AND ROY...
YOU BUILD YOUR FORT NEAR THE BRIDGE...
AND WE'LL MAKE OUR STAND THERE IF THE PARKSIDE KIDS ATTACK.
THE PLAN
BRIDGE
PARKSIDE
FORT
CAN WE PLAN OUR PATROL ROUTES?
YEAH, WE'VE GOT A LOT OF GROUND TO COVER!
SURE, I'LL GET SOME MORE PAPER!
HEY, WHY ISN'T SOPHIE WEARING HER COSTUME?
UM, IT'S A LONG STORY...
BE BACK IN A MINUTE!!

YOU NEED TO APOLOGIZE TO RAVEN.
YOU CRITICIZED EVERYTHING SHE SAID!
WHAT, BECAUSE I ASKED HER SOME QUESTIONS?
I'M SURE SHE'S A VERY NICE GIRL FOR SOMEONE ELSE...
BUT SHE'S WRONG FOR YOU.
YOU WERE NEVER EVEN GOING TO GIVE HER A CHANCE, WERE YOU?
AND YOU DON'T CARE AT ALL HOW MUCH THAT HURTS ME!
I--
SLAM!!!
SOPHIE!
UH, HI.
MOM SEEMS REALLY UPSET.

I THOUGHT YOUR MOTHER WOULD BE OVER THIS KIND OF TANTRUM BY NOW.
RAISING HER VOICE AT ME LIKE THAT...
BUT...
SO DISRESPECTFUL.
HEY, SOPHIE!
I HAD AN IDEA FOR--
AHH!!
MEEMAW!
WHOA! ARE YOU OKAY?
MY SWEATER IS RUINED!
I'M REALLY SORRY, MA'AM.
LET ME GET SOME PAPER TOWELS--
YOU'VE DONE ENOUGH ALREADY!
MEEMAW, HE DIDN'T MEAN TO...

DIDN'T ANYONE TEACH YOU MANNERS?!
IN MY DAY, CHILDREN BEHAVED!
THEY DIDN'T ACT LIKE LITTLE MONSTERS!
CLEARLY, YOUR MOTHER DIDN'T RAISE YOU PROPERLY!
BECAUSE--
LEAVE HIM ALONE!!!

I-- WHAT--
HEAD DOWNSTAIRS, ROY. I'LL DEAL WITH THIS.
OKAY, TH-THANKS.
SOPHIE, YOU CAN'T--
ROY IS MY FRIEND!
HE SAID SORRY!
YOU DON'T GET TO TALK TO HIM LIKE THAT!!
YOU DON'T GET TO TALK TO MOM LIKE THAT, EITHER!
RAVEN IS GREAT, AND I LIKE HER A LOT!
I'M HAPPY MOM HAS HER, AND YOU SHOULD BE HAPPY, TOO!!
AND I'M SORRY IF YOU DON'T LIKE ME BEING LOUD LIKE THIS...
BECAUSE LITTLE GIRLS SHOULD BE QUIET AND NICE, BUT...
BUT I'M THE BIG BANSHEE!
AND THE BIG BANSHEE STANDS UP FOR PEOPLE NO MATTER WHAT!

SOPHIE, I--
MOM!
IT'S FINE, HON. YOU DON'T HAVE TO--
NO, I **DO**.
MOTHER, I HAVE HAD **ENOUGH**.
RAVEN IS SPECIAL TO ME, AND YOU DON'T GET TO TREAT MY GIRLFRIEND LIKE--
I AGREE.
YOU... **WHAT**?
SOPHIE AND I JUST HAD A LITTLE...TALK.
AND I REALIZE I WAS **WRONG** TO JUDGE RAVEN SO HARSHLY.
I WASN'T FAIR TO **HER** OR TO **YOU**.

RAVEN, DEAR, I SEE HOW FIERCELY MY DAUGHTER CARES FOR YOU.
AND SOPHIE CLEARLY ADMIRES YOU.
I HOPE WE CAN START OVER.
I WOULD LOVE THAT.
NOW...
JUST **WHO** IS THIS **BIG BANSHEE** I'VE HEARD SO MUCH ABOUT?

a
Proclamation
of
Peace
Written and Illustrated by Chad Sell

PEOPLE OF PARKSIDE!
WE ARE HERE TO BRING PEACE TO OUR KINGDOMS!
WE MUST STOP **FIGHTING** AND SEE **REASON**!
a Proclamation of Peace
THE ONLY WAY FORWARD IS **TOGETHER**!
AND SO WE BRING YOU...THIS **PROCLAMATION OF PEACE**!

A "PROCLAMATION OF PEACE"? ARE YOU SERIOUS?
a Proclamation of Peace
YES, WE RESEARCHED HISTORICAL PEACE TREATIES IN ORDER TO--
I CAN'T EVEN READ THAT!
a Proclamation of Peace
IS IT WRITTEN IN ANOTHER LANGUAGE OR SOMETHING?
IT'S MY FINEST CALLIGRAPHY!
I ASSURE YOU THAT--
THEY'RE TRYING TO TRICK US INTO SIGNING SOMETHING WE CAN'T EVEN READ?!

WE'RE NOT TRYING TO TRICK ANYBODY!
IN FACT, WE THINK SOMEONE **ELSE** HAS TRICKED **ALL** OF US!
YES, WE'VE STUDIED THE EVIDENCE!
AND WE JUST NEED TIME TO FIGURE THIS OUT!
WHY DO YOU ALL WANT TO FIGHT SO BADLY?
IT'S **YOUR** SIDE THAT HAS BEEN BUILDING **FORTS** ALONG YOUR BORDER.
AND PATROLLING YOUR STREETS.
AND SENDING YOUR LITTLE DRONES TO SPY ON US!

BUT...
BUT YOU CAN'T POSSIBLY WIN AN ALL-OUT BATTLE AGAINST THE CARDBOARD KINGDOM!
IS THAT... A THREAT?
OF COURSE NOT!
BUT THERE ARE ONLY THREE OF YOU!
AGAINST OUR WHOLE NEIGHBORHOOD!
ONLY THREE? CAN'T YOU COUNT?!
ALL THE KIDS OF PARKSIDE WILL RISE UP AGAINST YOU!
AND TOGETHER, WE WILL CRUSH THE CARDBOARD KINGDOM!!!!

CRUSH! THE! KINGDOM!
CRUSH! THE! KINGDOM!
WHAT A DISASTER!
I... I REALLY THOUGHT THIS WAS MY BEST WORK!
IT'S BEAUTIFUL! BUT I GUESS IT WASN'T ENOUGH TO STOP THIS!
AT THIS POINT, IT'S HARD TO IMAGINE WHAT POSSIBLY COULD!
HOW FAR WILL THIS GO?
IS THERE ANY HOPE?
COME ON, TEAM!
BACK TO THE LAB!
INDEED!
TIME FOR SOME SERIOUS BRAINSTORMING!

THE
INVESTIGATOR
WRITTEN BY JASMINE WALLS
ILLUSTRATED BY CHAD SELL

ANOTHER CASE...
ANOTHER DARKENED DOORWAY.
BUT NO MATTER HOW DEEP THE SHADOWS ARE...
THE TRUTH WILL ALWAYS LIGHT THE WAY.
LET'S START WITH THE FACTS.

CLICK!
#1: GRANDPA LOST HIS GLASSES.
#2: MOM RECENTLY BOUGHT A NEW KIND OF DETERGENT.
AND #3:
GRANDPA ALWAYS TAKES OFF HIS GLASSES TO READ LABELS.
ALL THESE CLUES POINT TO ONE OBVIOUS ANSWER.

THE CASE OF THE MISSING GLASSES HAS BEEN **SOLVED**!
AND JUST IN TIME!
THE SHOW'S ABOUT TO START!
IT'S ALMOST FIVE, GRANDPA J. TIME FOR YOUR MEDICINE.
I WROTE IT DOWN SO WE WOULDN'T FORGET.
NOTHING GETS PAST YOU, DOES IT?
NO, SIR!
I BET I CAN GUESS THE CULPRIT BEFORE THE DETECTIVE DOES!
NOT IF I GUESS FIRST!
TRYING TO OUTDO THE PROFESSIONAL, HUH?
WE'LL SEE ABOUT THAT!

THIS CASE WENT COLD YEARS AGO...
BUT I JUST CAN'T SEEM TO LET IT GO.
I'M A LONE WOLF IN A HEARTLESS CITY.
I'M A LONE WOLF IN A HEARTLESS CITY.
HA HA! THAT WAS A GOOD IMPRESSION!
HA HA!
THESE SHOWS MAKE IT SEEM LIKE IT'S YOU AGAINST THE WORLD, BUT THAT'S NOT TRUE.
REALLY?
OH YES. I HIT THE STREETS AND KNOCKED ON PLENTY OF DOORS...
BUT I COULDN'T HAVE SOLVED THOSE CASES WITHOUT MY TEAM.
WHOA, YOU HAD BACKUP AS AN INVESTIGATOR?
YEP! MYSELF, SALLY, AND TOM.
I'VE GOT A PICTURE OF US UP IN MY ROOM.
I'LL SHOW YOU SOMETIME.

AT THE END OF THE EPISODE...
I WAS RIGHT. IT WAS THE LAWYER!
DANG IT.
THAT DIRTY SNEAK!
HELLO, YOU TWO.
HI, MOM!
HOW ABOUT YOU GO GET READY FOR DINNER? THEN YOU CAN TELL ME ALL ABOUT YOUR DAY!
MOMENTS LATER...
WHAT'S THIS?
THERE MUST HAVE BEEN A SECRET POCKET ON THE INSIDE!
J.S.T. SALES? HMM.
J.S.T. SALES
TRINI, ARE YOU READY?
COMING!

HOW WAS YOUR DAY, TRINI? ANY EXCITING NEW CASES?
YEAH!
SOMETHING'S BREWING BETWEEN PARKSIDE AND THE CARDBOARD KINGDOM.
SOMETHING... **SINISTER**.
BUT I HAVEN'T BEEN ABLE TO WORK IT ALL OUT YET.
THAT **DOES** SOUND LIKE A BIG CASE.
WHAT WAS THAT ABOUT A **KINGDOM**?
APPARENTLY, THE KIDS HAVE THIS WHOLE BIG GAME, WITH CHARACTERS AND EVERYTHING.
THAT'S NICE. I'M GLAD YOU'RE OUT MAKING FRIENDS, PUMPKIN.
NO MAKE-BELIEVE FOR **TRINI**, THOUGH.
SHE'S A **REAL DETECTIVE**, THROUGH AND THROUGH.
JUST LIKE **YOU**, GRANDPA J!

THE NEXT MORNING...
G'MORNING!
DON'T FORGET TO TAKE YOUR PILLS WITH BREAKFAST.
ALREADY DID!
BUT I CAN'T SEEM TO FIND MY FAVORITE MUG.
I WANTED TO MAKE SOME COFFEE.
AND THE COFFEEPOT SEEMS TO HAVE GONE MISSING AS WELL.
I'LL HELP YOU FIND THEM.
THEY'VE GOTTA BE AROUND HERE SOMEWHERE.
I'LL CHECK THE DISHWASHER.
I'LL CHECK THE OTHER ROOM, JUST IN CASE.
FOUND THEM!
HMM.

YOUR MOTHER MUST HAVE LEFT IT FOR ME BEFORE HEADING TO WORK.
JUST NEEDS A LITTLE MILK AND IT'LL BE PERFECT.
MOM WENT TO WORK EARLY TODAY.
SHE MUST HAVE LEFT HOURS AGO.
SO...
WHY IS THE COFFEE STILL HOT?
FIRST THE GLASSES AND NOW THIS?
GRANDPA J IS FORGETTING THINGS EVEN MORE THAN USUAL.

LATER...
WHAT IS THIS CARD?
AND WHY WAS IT IN A SECRET POCKET IN GRANDPA J'S OLD COAT?
J.S.T.?
SOUNDS KIND OF FAMILIAR.
MAYBE THEY'RE INITIALS?
WE CAN SELL ANYTHING!
WHOA, YOU HAD BACKUP AS AN INVESTIGATOR?
YEP! MYSELF, SALLY, AND TOM.
I'VE GOT A PICTURE OF US UP IN MY ROOM.
I'LL SHOW YOU SOMETIME.
THE NAMES FIT, BUT...THAT CAN'T BE RIGHT.
GRANDPA WAS A **DETECTIVE**.
J.→ GRANDPA J
S.→ SALLY
T.→ TOM
THE **PHOTO**!
GRANDPA J SAID HE HAD A PHOTO WITH HIS TEAM!
MAYBE IT'LL HAVE MORE CLUES.

SORRY, GRANDPA J...
BUT I'VE GOT TO FIND THE **TRUTH**!
OUR FIRST BIG DAY OF SALES!
I HIT THE STREETS AND KNOCKED ON PLENTY OF DOORS...
HE WASN'T A DETECTIVE AT ALL.
HE WASN'T OUT COLLECTING **CLUES**...
HE WAS JUST SELLING **VACUUMS**.

EARLY THAT EVENING...
HOW WAS YOUR DAY, PUMPKIN?
SOLVE ANY NEW MYSTERIES?
...ONLY ONE.
I'M SURE SHE'S JUST TIRED.
SHE'S BEEN RUNNING AROUND CHASING LEADS AND CRACKING CASES WIDE OPEN!
WELL, IF YOU'RE DONE EATING...
YOU CAN GO WATCH A SHOW WITH YOUR GRANDPA WHILE I WASH UP.
NO THANKS, I **AM** PRETTY TIRED.
OH, ALRIGHT, THEN.
I'LL BE UP SOON TO SAY GOOD NIGHT.

PUMPKIN, ARE YOU OKAY?
YOU DIDN'T SEEM LIKE YOURSELF AT DINNER.
I FOUND THIS IN GRANDPA J'S COAT.
WHY WOULD HE LIE ABOUT BEING A DETECTIVE?
OH.
WELL, UH...
TRINI, YOUR GRANDPA ISN'T LYING TO YOU.
NOT EXACTLY.
WHAT DO YOU MEAN? WAS HE UNDERCOVER?
OR A SECRET AGENT?
YOU KNOW HOW GRANDPA FORGETS THINGS?
WELL, HE ALSO GETS... CONFUSED.
HE MIXES UP THE THINGS HE WATCHES WITH HIS REAL MEMORIES.

SO IT'S BECAUSE HE WATCHES SO MANY DETECTIVE SHOWS...
AND READS ALL THOSE MYSTERY BOOKS.
YOU'RE RIGHT.
I THOUGHT I WAS BEING A GOOD DETECTIVE, JUST LIKE GRANDPA J.
BUT IT WAS ALL JUST... MAKE-BELIEVE.
IF I'M NOT A **REAL** DETECTIVE, HOW AM I SUPPOSED TO HELP GRANDPA J?
HE KEEPS FORGETTING THINGS MORE AND MORE!
I'M SORRY, PUMPKIN.
I'VE BEEN WORKING SO MUCH, I DIDN'T SEE WHAT YOU'VE BEEN DEALING WITH.
YOU'RE SUCH A GOOD DETECTIVE. THAT HASN'T CHANGED.
YOU'VE SOLVED **SO** MANY CASES, YOU **MUST** BE THE REAL DEAL.

SOMETIMES LEARNING THE TRUTH DOESN'T GET YOU THE ANSWERS YOU WANT TO HEAR.
YEAH, SOMETIMES THE TRUTH REALLY STINKS!
DO YOU THINK YOU'D BE BETTER OFF IF YOU NEVER FOUND OUT?
NO, EVEN IF IT HURTS...
IT'S BETTER TO KNOW.
I GUESS THAT'S WHY DETECTIVES ALWAYS LOOK SO TOUGH.
THAT'S RIGHT.
AND YOU'RE THE TOUGHEST ONE I KNOW.

THE NEXT MORNING...
YOU DIDN'T GO TO WORK YET, MOM?
I'VE WORKED A LOT OF EXTRA HOURS RECENTLY.
I CAN AFFORD TO TAKE A FEW MORNINGS OFF EACH WEEK.
HAS ANYONE SEEN MY FAVORITE MUG?
IT'S ON THE TABLE, DAD.
I CAN TAKE CARE OF THINGS HERE, TRINI.
WHY DON'T YOU GO SOLVE THAT BIG CASE?

WATCH OUT, TROUBLEMAKERS!
THE INVESTIGATOR IS BACK ON THE CASE!

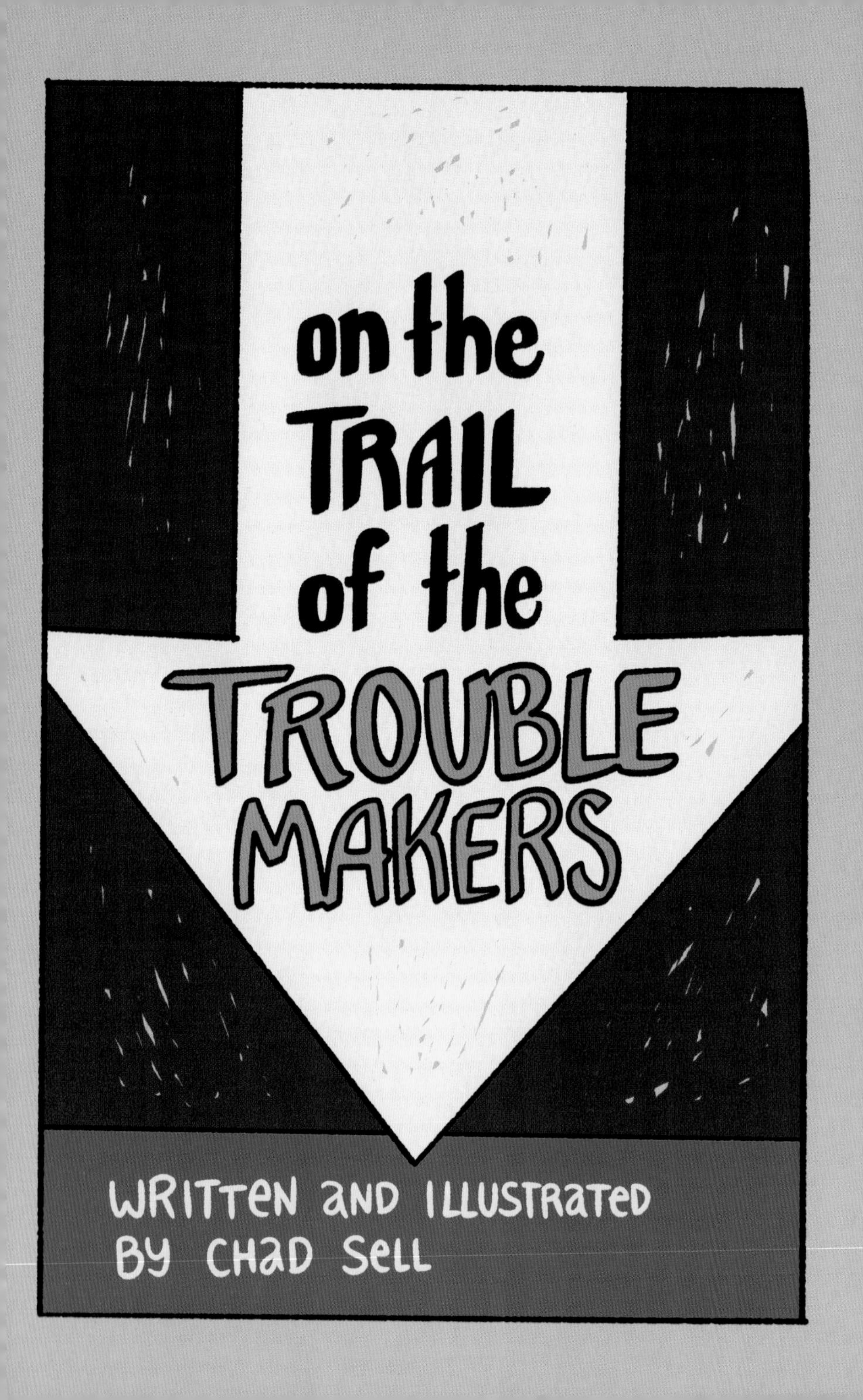
on the
TRAIL
of the
TROUBLE
MAKERS
WRITTEN AND ILLUSTRATED
BY CHAD SELL

THAT NIGHT IN PARKSIDE...
WHAT IF THOSE CARDBOARD KINGDOM KIDS SHOW UP AGAIN?
WE FIGHT THEM OFF! TOGETHER!
BUT THEY HAVE COSTUMES!
AND WEAPONS!
I CAN MAKE YOU COSTUMES JUST LIKE THEIRS!
I CAN COPY ANYTHING THEY'VE GOT!
I'LL MAKE YOU WHATEVER YOU WANT!
IF YOU JOIN... THE COPYCAT'S KITTY CLONES!!
OOOH!
COOL!!
KITTY CLONES?
HA!
MORE LIKE...
SCAREDY-CATS.
A SPY!
AHHHH!!!!!

I--
I'M NOT A SPY!
I WASN'T SPYING!
YOU ARE, AND YOU WERE.
SEE ANYTHING INTERESTING?
I THOUGHT YOU WORKED ALONE.
USED TO. BUT I CAN'T CRACK THIS CASE MYSELF.
WHAT CASE?
I'M ON THE TRAIL OF THE TROUBLEMAKER WHO DREAMED UP ALL THIS NEIGHBORHOOD DRAMA.
YOU THINK ONE PERSON IS BEHIND IT ALL?
WELL, I KNOW SOMEBODY SMASHED YOUR SNOW SCULPTURES IN THE PARK.
AND THEN SOMEBODY ELSE TOOK DOWN VALKYRIE.
BUT I KEEP ASKING MYSELF THIS ONE THING...
WHAT IF THEY WERE BOTH THE SAME PERSON?

IF WE COULD **PROVE** THAT THIS WHOLE THING IS PART OF SOMEBODY'S SCHEME...
WOULD IT MAKE A DIFFERENCE?
IT WOULD **HAVE** TO, RIGHT?
BUT WHERE'S THE PROOF?
CHECK WITH YOUR SCIENCE SQUAD.
SEE IF THEY GOT SOME FOOTPRINTS IN THE PARK FROM THE SNOW SMASHER.
I...THINK THEY **DID**.
BUT...
WHAT THEN?
WILL WE HAVE TO CHECK EVERYONE'S BOOTS UNTIL WE FIND A MATCH?
NOT IF THE PRINTS MATCH THE ONES I FOUND AT THE CRIME SCENE WHEN VALKYRIE WAS ATTACKED.
AH HA!
THAT'S IT!!
I'LL CHECK WITH THEM RIGHT AWAY!
GOOD WORK, INVESTIGATOR!
THANKS.

LET ME KNOW WHAT YOU FIND OUT.
AND MAYBE WE CAN CLOSE THIS CASE BEFORE...
BEFORE...
HA!
AND HE SAYS HE'S NOT A SPY...

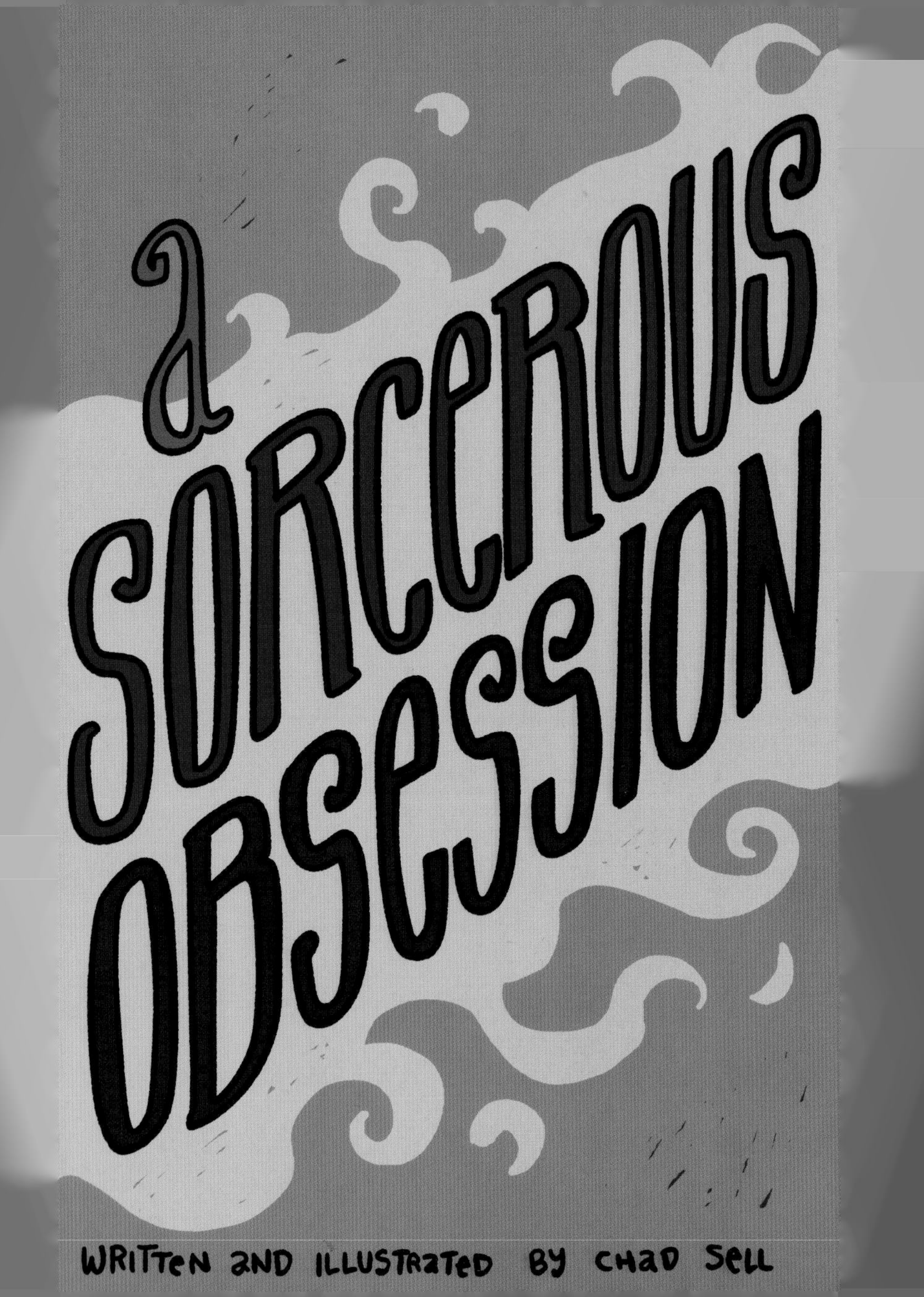
a Sorcerous Obsession
Written and illustrated by Chad Sell

PERRRRFECT.
JACK, IT'S NOT THAT COLD OUTSIDE.
WHAT ARE YOU DOING?
IT'S A CLOAKING SPELL.
FOR A VERY HUSH-HUSH SECRET MISSION.
WHAT ARE ALL OF YOU DOING?
IS IT FOR THE--
SHHH! HUSH-HUSH SECRET MISSION STUFF!
OH.
WELL...
GOOD.

JACK?
IS THAT YOU?!
IT'S HARD TO TELL BECAUSE OF MY CLOAKING SPELL, RIGHT?
CLOAKING SPELL?
SERIOUSLY...
WHAT ARE YOU UP TO?
WHAT ARE YOU DOING IN PARKSIDE?

I'M ON A SECRET MISSION!
TO SPY ON THAT RIP-OFF WANNABE--
THE NECROMANCER?
OF COURSE. YOU'RE OBSESSED WITH HER.
WHAT?!
OBSESSED?
NO, I...
THERE CAN ONLY BE ONE EVIL MISTRESS OF MAGIC IN THE LAND!
WHY?
UM. BECAUSE, UH...
BECAUSE YOU DON'T WANT TO SHARE THE SPOTLIGHT WITH ANYBODY ELSE.
THAT'S-- THAT'S NOT FAIR!
AND IT'S NOT TRUE!
JUST BE CAREFUL, JACK.
THERE'S SOME SERIOUS STUFF GOING ON.
AND YOU'RE NOT INVISIBLE, YOU KNOW.

A LITTLE WHILE LATER...
THE SORCERESS!
SHE MUST BE DEFEATED!!
BUT ONLY I CAN DISPEL HER DARK MAGIC!
JOIN MY SKELETON CREW! I'LL MAKE YOU UNDEAD AND UNSTOPPABLE!
THE NECROMANCER IS RECRUITING?
AND... USING ME TO DO IT?
BUT...
WHAT'S SO SCARY ABOUT THE SORCERESS?
SHE'S THE MOST POWERFUL MAGE IN THE CARDBOARD KINGDOM!
IT'S HER SINISTER SCHEMES AND SPELLS THAT IMPERIL ALL OF PARKSIDE!
BUT I CAN STOP HER!
WITH YOUR HELP!

THE MOST POWERFUL?
I'M REALLY THE **BIGGEST THREAT** TO PARKSIDE?
ME?!
IT'S ALMOST LIKE...
IS...
IS THE NECROMANCER OBSESSED WITH **ME**?!
YOU?!
IT'S HER!! **THE SORCERESS**!
STAND BACK, EVERYONE!
SHE'S DANGEROUS!
BUT I CAN HANDLE HER.
UH-OH.

WHY HAVE YOU COME HERE?
AND WHY ARE YOU DRESSED LIKE THAT?
UH...
IT WAS A CLOAKING-- NEVER MIND.
ARE YOU HERE TO CHALLENGE ME TO A SORCERY SHOWDOWN?
A TEST OF OUR MAGICAL MIGHT?!
WHAT?!
HERE? NOW?!
I'M NOT EVEN IN COSTUME!
AND THERE'S BARELY ANYONE HERE!
WHAT DO YOU MEAN?
WHY...
WHY WOULD THAT MATTER?

IF WE'RE GOING TO HAVE A **REAL** SHOWDOWN, DON'T YOU WANT EVERYONE TO **SEE** IT?
TO SEE US BOTH AT OUR **BEST**?
HUH, YEAH.
IT COULD BE **SPECTACULAR**!
RIGHT?! WE WOULD NEED, LIKE...**MUSIC**!
AND COSTUME CHANGES!
CHOREOGRAPHY!
SPECIAL EFFECTS!
BUT... THAT'S A LOT TO FIGURE OUT.
IT WOULD TAKE **A TON** OF PLANNING TO DO IT RIGHT.
YEAH, HMM...
I HAVE AN IDEA.
BUT WE'LL NEED TO KEEP IT VERY... **HUSH-HUSH**.

LATER...
SAM?
ARE YOU STILL UP THERE DOING SECRET STUFF WITH EVERYBODY?
NO!!!
DUNGEON OF HORRORS ENTER IF YOU DARE!
PERRRRFECT.
DING-DONG!

HI.
HEY.
YOU LOOK SO...
WHAT?
NORMAL?
CAN I COME IN? BEFORE ANYBODY SEES?
RIGHT, OF COURSE.
NO ONE CAN KNOW WHAT WE'RE DOING.
NOT EVEN YOUR LITTLE MINION OR WHATEVER.
SHE'S MY SISTER AND ASSOCIATE, BUT YES.
THIS STAYS BETWEEN YOU AND ME.
PERRRRFECT.

SOON AFTER...
OKAY, SO...
AFTER YOU CAST YOUR BLIZZARD BLAST...
THE SNOW WILL FALL AWAY TO REVEAL I'VE BEEN TRANSFORMED INTO AN INCREDIBLE **ICE QUEEN**...
AND THEN...
WAIT, WILL YOU HAVE **TIME** FOR THAT COSTUME CHANGE?
SURE, DURING YOUR BIG SPEECH.
OKAY!
THEN I'LL SUMMON MY STORM OF ICICLES...
YEAH!
YOU GET ME WITH THOSE, AND...
I'LL SPIT OUT SOME STRAWBERRY JAM SO IT RUNS DOWN MY **CHIN**.
EW, **GROSS**!
IT'LL LOOK JUST LIKE **BLOOD**!
LET'S...MARK THAT AS A "MAYBE."

HEY, KIDS!
JACK, WHO'S YOUR FRIEND?
WE'RE NOT FRIENDS.
WE ARE MAGICAL RIVALS.
OKAY, WELL, HI! I'M JACK'S MOM.
UM, I'M NANDO.
GOOD TO MEET YOU!
WHAT ARE YOU TWO WORKING ON?
OH, NOTHING, WE...
WE'RE PLANNING A SHOWDOWN!
THE SORCERESS VERSUS THE NECROMANCER!
EVERYONE WILL LITERALLY BE TALKING ABOUT IT FOR THE REST OF THEIR LIVES.
RIGHT, NANDO?

HUH.
THIS IS... A LOT.
WHERE ARE YOU GOING TO FIND A CONFETTI CANNON?
WE'RE...STILL WORKING IT ALL OUT.
WELL, GOOD THING YOU'VE FOUND A NICE NEW FRIEND TO HELP!
MAGICAL RIVAL!
SURE, SWEETIE!
LET ME KNOW IF YOU NEED ANYTHING!
SHE...
SHE KNOWS ABOUT THE SORCERESS?
WHAT?
YEAH, OF COURSE.
WHY?

DOESN'T YOUR...?
OH.
YOUR FAMILY DOESN'T KNOW ABOUT...THE NECROMANCER?
THEY... WOULDN'T REALLY GET WHAT I'M DOING.
AND THEY DEFINITELY WOULDN'T LIKE IT.
WELL...
I DO.
HUH?
I LIKE WHAT YOU'RE DOING.
YOUR COSTUME IS SOOO COOL! THAT CAPE? SERIOUSLY?!
AND I WISH I COULD PULL OFF THAT EYE MAKEUP.
THANKS.
IT'S JUST FACE PAINT. IT'S NOT ANYTHING SPECIAL.
IT IS.
IT REALLY IS.

SO, UH...
HOW DOES OUR BIG BATTLE END?
WHO WINS?
HUH.
MAYBE WE BOTH CAN?
BUT... BUT WE'RE RIVALS!
IT CAN'T JUST END IN A TIE!
WELL, WHAT IF WE COULD SHOW EVERYBODY THAT, UH...
THAT EVEN RIVALS CAN OVERCOME THEIR DIFFERENCES AND DO SOMETHING MAGICAL AND AMAZING?
THAT WE'RE EVEN MORE POWERFUL TOGETHER?
THAT SOUNDS GREAT, BUT IT WILL HAVE TO BE QUITE A SHOW TO CONVINCE EVERYONE.
SO...
WE'LL DEFINITELY NEED MORE FAKE BLOOD.

YEAH...
THAT'S STILL GOING TO BE A "MAYBE."

the Secret WEAPONS LAB
WRITTEN BY JAY FULLER-NG
ILLUSTRATED BY CHAD SELL

ALRIGHT, THE SORCERESS ASKED US TO MAKE DEVIOUS NEW WEAPONS TO SPRING ON THOSE PARKSIDE KIDS!
SO LET'S SHOW THEM WHAT HAPPENS WHEN THEY MESS WITH US!
WHAT HAVE ALL OF YOU BEEN WORKING ON?
I MADE A MIGHTY MEGAPHONE TO MAGNIFY MY BLOODCURDLING ROAR!
RARRR!!
NOT BAD, BEAST!
THAT WILL DEFINITELY SCARE THEM A BIT...
BUT I THINK WE NEED A LITTLE MORE.

HOW ABOUT YOU, CONNIE?
THIS IS A COMPUTER VIRUS THAT NO ARTIFICIAL INTELLIGENCE CAN WITHSTAND.
OBSERVE.
MY CIRCUITS ARE MALFUNCTIONING!
CANNOT WITHSTAND!
HA!
THAT'LL BE GOOD AGAINST ROBOTS, I GUESS, BUT...
WHAT ABOUT EVERYONE ELSE?

ELIJAH, DID YOU MAKE ANYTHING?
I...DON'T THINK IT'S READY.
WHAT IS IT?
I DON'T KNOW.
HOW DO YOU USE IT?
I DON'T KNOW!!
OKAY, WELL...
LET ME SHOW YOU WHAT I'VE BEEN WORKING ON.

IT'S A MACHINE FOR MAKING SNOWBALLS!
TONS OF THEM!
ALL YOU DO IS ADD ICE UP HERE...
SPIN THIS KNOB TO GRIND IT ALL UP...
AND EVENTUALLY YOU'LL HAVE ENOUGH SNOW TO MAKE A BUNCH OF SNOWBALLS AT ONCE!

BUT...
WHY DON'T YOU JUST USE THE SNOW **OUTSIDE**?
BECAUSE, UH...
ELIJAH, YOU'RE A **GENIUS**!
THEY'RE STILL ONLY SNOWBALLS, THOUGH.
I THOUGHT WE WANTED SOMETHING... **IMPRESSIVE**.
ANY PUNY HUMAN CAN MAKE A SNOWBALL WITH THEIR FEEBLE LITTLE HANDS.
HMM...
YOU'RE RIGHT. WE HAVE TO THINK **BIGGER**.
JACK IS COUNTING ON US.
THE **WHOLE KINGDOM** IS COUNTING ON US.

WHAT IF WE MIXED IN YOUR STINKY SLIME?
WE COULD MAKE A MILLION SLIMEBALLS WITH YOUR MACHINE!
HA HA! STINKY, SLIMY SNOWBALLS?!
WE'RE ALL EVIL GENIUSES!
MWAHAHA!
BUT... HMM.
THIS ISN'T ENOUGH SLIME.
WE CAN HELP MAKE MORE!
WE CAN MAKE IT EVEN SLIMIER AND STINKIER!
YES! HUMANS HATE STINKY SMELLS!
YES, PERFECT!
LET'S GET STARTED!

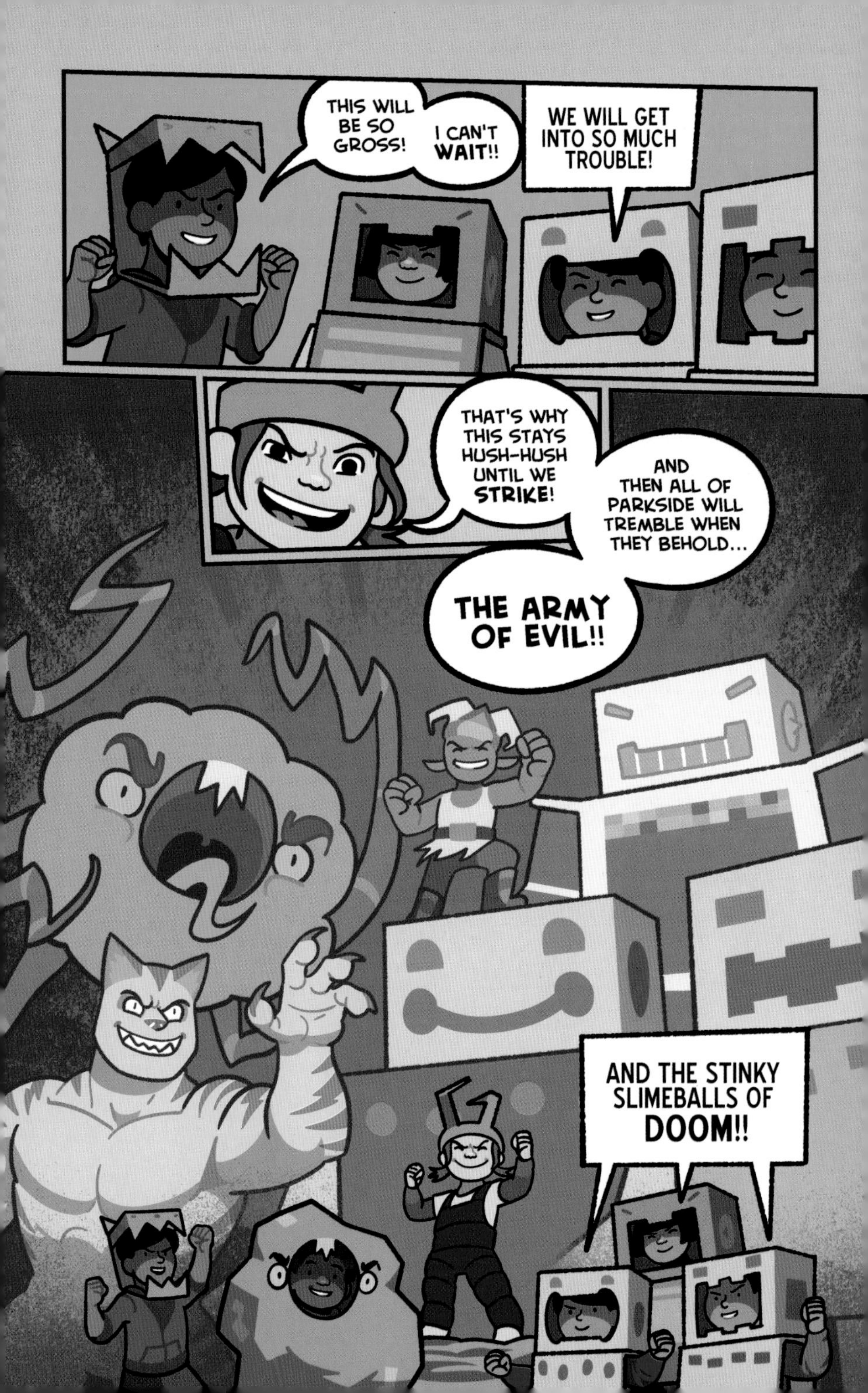
THIS WILL BE SO GROSS!
I CAN'T WAIT!!
WE WILL GET INTO SO MUCH TROUBLE!
THAT'S WHY THIS STAYS HUSH-HUSH UNTIL WE STRIKE!
AND THEN ALL OF PARKSIDE WILL TREMBLE WHEN THEY BEHOLD...
THE ARMY OF EVIL!!
AND THE STINKY SLIMEBALLS OF DOOM!!

FINISHING
the
FORT
WRITTEN BY JAY FULLER-NG
ILLUSTRATED BY CHAD SELL

WOW, PETE!
THIS FORT IS STARTING TO LOOK JUST LIKE THE DESIGN YOU SKETCHED!

WILL IT BE READY FOR THE BIG BATTLE JACK'S BEEN TALKING ABOUT?
BETWEEN BOTH OF OUR NEIGHBORHOODS?
HEY, BOYS!
WE CAME TO CHECK OUT THE FORT!
AND TO SEE IF YOU MIGHT WANT TO FORT-IFY YOURSELVES WITH SOME HOT CHOCOLATE!
TWENTY-FIVE GOLD A CUP!
TWENTY-FIVE GOLD?
UH...SORRY, I DON'T REALLY HAVE ANY.
WHAT?
DOESN'T YOUR GRANDMA GIVE YOU AN ALLOWANCE?
SHE DID.
BUT NOW THAT I'M STAYING WITH MY MOM...
OH.

WAIT, UM...
I FORGOT!
WE HAVE A SPECIAL DEAL TODAY:
BUY ONE, GET ONE FREE!
RIGHT! SURE!
THAT'S OKAY. THANKS, THOUGH.
BUT...
ACTUALLY, I GOTTA GO FINISH SOME STUFF BEFORE MY MOM GETS HOME.
I'M SORRY I CAN'T HELP WITH THE FORT, PETE.
MAYBE I CAN COME BACK LATER?

HEY, LOOK!
THE PARKSIDE KIDS ARE BUILDING A SNOW FORT, TOO!
WHAT?!
DON'T WORRY, PETER.
YOURS WILL BE WAY COOLER. PUN INTENDED.
HEY! ROYZILLA! SMASH UP THEIR FORT REAL GOOD!
WHAT, DIDN'T HE HEAR ME?
IS HE... HELPING THEM?!

PETER, YOU KNOW ROY BETTER THAN ANYONE.
DO YOU THINK HE WOULD EVER SWITCH SIDES?
SHAKE
THEN...
THEN WHY DID HE REFUSE MY AMAZING HOT CHOCOLATE AND JUST TAKE THEIR CRUMMY COLD CHOCOLATE?!
IT LOOKS PRETTY BAD...
DOESN'T IT, PETER?

IF ROYZILLA JOINS THEIR ARMY, THEY'LL BE UNSTOPPABLE!
UH-OH, THAT RICH GUY IS COMING THIS WAY!
HE'S GOT SOME NERVE...
HEY, KID.
YOUR FRIEND ROY TELLS ME **YOU'RE** THE ONE WHO PLANNED OUT THIS **MAGNIFICENT** SNOW FORT.
IS THAT TRUE?

WHY DON'T WE MAKE A DEAL?
COME WORK FOR ME, AND AS A SIGNING BONUS...
MR. MILLIONAIRE
I'LL GIVE YOU AN ORIGINAL, KING-SIZE...
MR. MILLIONAIRE CANDY BAR.
HE HAS HIS OWN CANDY BAR??
HE...HE HAS HIS OWN CANDY BAR!!
COME ON, DITCH THESE CARDBOARD DORKS!
JOIN THE WINNING TEAM!

MR. MILLIONAIRE
HE REJECTS YOUR OFFER!
AND SO DO I!
I MEAN... IF YOU WERE OFFERING, I WOULD REJECT IT.
...ARE YOU MAKING AN OFFER?
NO.
THEN GET OUTTA HERE!
ALRIGHT, KID.
IF YOU COME TO YOUR SENSES LIKE YOUR FRIEND ROY, YOU KNOW WHERE TO FIND US...
THE COOL SIDE OF TOWN.

ARE YOU KIDDING ME? WHO TALKS LIKE THAT?
AND HOW CAN HE AFFORD TO GIVE OUT KING-SIZE CANDY BARS LIKE... LIKE THEY'RE CANDY?!
I CAN'T BELIEVE ROY WOULD HELP HIM OF ALL PEOPLE.
COME ON, BECKY.
WE NEED TO FIND OUT MORE ABOUT THIS SO-CALLED MILLIONAIRE.
I'M SORRY ABOUT ROY, PETER.

AARGGH!!
OWW!!
AAHHH!!!

AAAHHHH!!

A SHORT WHILE LATER...
OH MY GOSH! PETE!
I HURRIED BACK AS SOON AS I FINISHED MY CHORES.
WHAT HAPPENED?
WHY ARE YOU SO UPSET?
OH...
THAT GUY CAME BY, HUH?
LOOK... I KNOW THINGS HAVE BEEN DIFFERENT NOW THAT I LIVE IN PARKSIDE.
AND I'M SORRY I'VE BEEN SO BUSY AT MY MOM'S...
BUT, PETE...
I'D **NEVER** SELL YOU OUT FOR A **CANDY BAR**.

I KNOW SOME THINGS ARE BEST LEFT UNSAID, BUT...
I'LL **ALWAYS** COME BACK TO THE CARDBOARD KINGDOM.
'CUZ THAT'S WHERE MY BEST FRIEND LIVES, PETE.

NOW, UH...
HOW ABOUT WE FINISH UP THAT FORT?

CRUSHING
the
COMPETITION
WRITTEN AND ILLUSTRATED BY CHAD SELL

BECKY, WE'RE IN TROUBLE.
FIRST MR. MILLIONAIRE BRIBED ALL THOSE KIDS WITH CANDY TO BUILD HIM THAT SNOW PALACE...
NOW HE'S SUITING THEM UP WITH, WITH--WHATEVER **THOSE** ARE!
THEY'RE MECH SUITS! WITH BLASTERS AND STUFF!
I DON'T KNOW WHO DESIGNED THEM, BUT THEY'RE **AMAZING**!
THOSE PARKSIDE KIDS REALLY KNOW WHAT THEY'RE DOING!
HMPH!

WITH ALL THAT CANDY, MR. MILLIONAIRE CAN GET KIDS TO DO WHATEVER HE WANTS!
SO THAT'S WHAT WE NEED TO FIGURE OUT.
WHERE DOES HE GET IT?
CUT HIM OFF FROM HIS CANDY SUPPLY, AND WE'LL CRUSH HIM!!
MWAHAHA!!!
YOU KNOW, ALICE, I'VE BEEN THINKING...
REMEMBER HOW YOU AND I GOT OFF TO A BAD START LAST SUMMER?
AND WE SORT OF GOT CARRIED AWAY COMPETING WITH EACH OTHER FOR BUSINESS?
IT WAS GLORIOUS!
I DON'T QUITE REMEMBER IT THAT WAY, BUT...
WHAT I'M SAYING IS...
YOU DON'T HAVE TO SEE EVERYBODY AS EITHER CUSTOMERS OR COMPETITION.
WHAT ARE YOU GETTING AT, BECKY?

WASN'T EVERYTHING SO MUCH **BETTER** WHEN WE STARTED THE DRAGON'S HEAD INN TOGETHER?
WHEN WE STOPPED **COMPETING** AND STARTED **COOPERATING** AS--
AS BUSINESS PARTNERS?
AS **FRIENDS,** ALICE.
OKAY, FINE, YOU'RE RIGHT.
BUT YOU CAN'T EXPECT ME TO WORK WITH MR. MILLIONAIRE!
HE'S ARROGANT AND LOUD AND ENTITLED. LIKE, LIKE--
LIKE **YOU**?
IF YOU WOULD WORK ON YOUR **PEOPLE SKILLS,** ALICE...
MAYBE YOU WOULDN'T **ALWAYS** GET OFF TO SUCH A **BAD START** WITH FOLKS.
THIS ISN'T ABOUT **ME,** BECKY!
THIS IS ABOUT BEATING MR. MILLIONAIRE AND HIS MECHANICAL CRONIES!

HEY, NERDS!
I NEED TO TALK TO THE NEW GIRL!
WHO, ME?
HER NAME IS LA MECÁNICA, AND SHE IS NOT A NERD!
NO, I AM! IT'S OKAY!
BUT IT'S NOT OKAY TO TALK TO YOU LIKE THAT!
PEOPLE SKILLS, ALICE.
HRM.
I-- LOOK, SORRY.
WE GOT OFF TO A BAD START.
I WANTED TO ASK ABOUT MR. MILLIONAIRE. DO YOU KNOW HIM?

WHO, MIKHAIL?
YEAH, HE'S REALLY NOT SO BAD.
BUT WHERE DOES HE GET ALL HIS CANDY? ARE HIS PARENTS RICH OR SOMETHING?
RICH? I DON'T THINK SO. THEY RUN A CONVENIENCE STORE IN PARKSIDE.
WAIT, MR. MILLIONAIRE'S PARENTS RUN...
A CONVENIENCE STORE?!
YEAH, IT'S REALLY NICE! THEY'VE GOT EVERYTHING THERE!
LIKE... CANDY?
OF COURSE!
THAT'S DEFINITELY WORTH CHECKING OUT!
THANKS SOOO MUCH, ISABELA!
I LIKE YOUR BRAIDS!
THANKS! BYE!

A SHORT WHILE LATER...
DING!
WOW...
BECKY, THIS PLACE...
IT IS REALLY NICE.
SO NICE!
LOOK! THEY HAVE CHIPS!
AND CHURROS!
AND WARM COOKIES?!
OVER HERE! LOOK!
OH!
THOSE ARE THE CANDY BARS MR. MILLIONAIRE HAS BEEN GIVING AWAY!
BUT THEY'RE ALMOST GONE!
MR. MILLIONAIRE
MR. MILLIONAIRE

MIKHAIL HAS BEEN STEALING FROM HIS OWN FAMILY!
YOU DON'T KNOW THAT, ALICE!
HI, GIRLS. CAN I HELP YOU WITH ANYTHING?
BUT I CAN PROVE IT, BECKY.
WHAT? HOW?
OH! UM, WELL...
HI, SIR. MY FRIEND AND I BOTH WANTED TO GET A MR. MILLIONAIRE CANDY BAR...
BUT IT LOOKS LIKE YOU ONLY HAVE ONE LEFT.
MR. MILLIONAIRE
HUH, THAT'S STRANGE.
I SWEAR MY SON JUST RESTOCKED THOSE.
BUT WE SHOULD HAVE MORE IN THE BACK!
I'LL GO LOOK.
OH GOSH, THAT WOULD BE SOOOO NICE! THANKS!

ALICE! WHAT ARE YOU DOING?!
WHAT IF THERE'S NO MORE CANDY BACK THERE?
THEN WE'VE GOT THE PROOF WE NEED.
BUT MIKHAIL WILL GET IN SO MUCH TROUBLE!!
I KNOW. IT'S THRILLING, RIGHT?
WE'RE ON THE VERGE OF VICTORY!
BUT HOW WILL HIS PARENTS FEEL?
TO FIND OUT THAT THEIR SON HAS BEEN STEALING FROM THEM?
THEY... THEY'LL BE CRUSHED!
YEAH, BUT-- BUT...

I'M SORRY, GIRLS, I DIDN'T FIND ANY MORE.
BUT I COULD ASK MY SON IF HE KNOWS WHERE THEY COULD BE.
HE **LOVES** THOSE CANDY BARS.
UMMM...
UHHHH...
DON'T WORRY ABOUT IT!
HUH?
WE CAN JUST SHARE THIS ONE. RIGHT, BECKY?
SURE! RIGHT! YEAH!
MR. MILLIONAIRE
BECAUSE... I LOVE... SHARING?

ONE QUICK TRANSACTION LATER...
DING!
I... BUT... ALICE!
I THOUGHT THAT THE WHOLE PLAN WAS TO--
WE NEED A NEW PLAN, BECKY.
WHY?
BECAUSE YOU WERE RIGHT.
MIKHAIL'S DAD SEEMS NICE, AND... I DON'T WANT TO CRUSH HIM.
SO...SO WE NEED A PLAN WHERE WE ALL WIN.
EVERYBODY.
EVEN...UGH... MR. MILLIONAIRE.

THAT SOUNDS GREAT, BUT...
HOW?
REMEMBER, BECKY?
PEOPLE SKILLS.
AW, ALICE!!
YOU--YOU LISTENED!!
YEAH, YEAH.
NOW COME ON, BECKY!
LET'S GET DOWN TO BUSINESS!!
HA HA, YAY!
MMM!

BEHIND enemy LINES

WRITTEN BY MANUEL BETANCOURT
ILLUSTRATED BY CHAD SELL

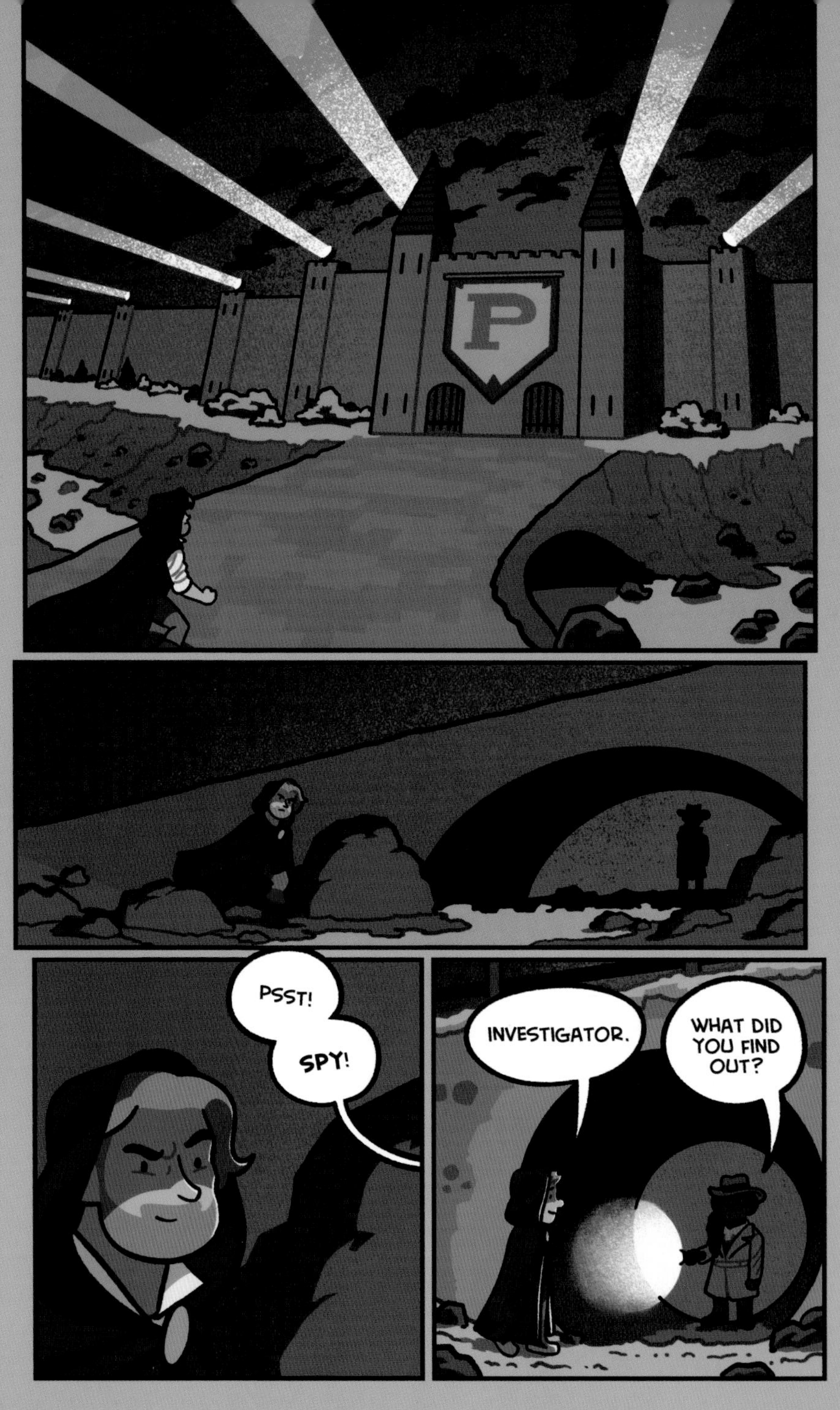
P
PSST!
SPY!
INVESTIGATOR.
WHAT DID YOU FIND OUT?

YOU WERE RIGHT.
THE SNOW SMASHER WAS THE SAME KID WHO ATTACKED VALKYRIE.
YUP.
THE BOOT PRINTS MATCH.
SO SOMEONE WANTED KIDS IN BOTH KINGDOMS TO SUSPECT EACH OTHER.
TO FIGHT.
YEAH, I HEAR YOU'RE DIGGING IN FOR A BIG BATTLE WITH PARKSIDE TOMORROW.
WHAT?!
I'VE HEARD PARKSIDE IS GETTING READY TO ATTACK!
HMM...IT HASN'T TAKEN VERY MUCH FOR EVERYONE TO GET CARRIED AWAY WITH ALL THIS, HAS IT?
CARRIED AWAY?
WE HAVE TO DEFEND OURSELVES! OUR KINGDOM!!
DON'T YOU THINK EVERYBODY IN PARKSIDE IS SAYING THE SAME THING?

I...
I JUST CAN'T FIGURE OUT WHY SOMEONE WOULD WANT ALL OF US TO FIGHT.
AGREED.
WE DON'T HAVE A MOTIVE YET.
BUT I'VE GOT A GOOD GUESS WHO'S BEHIND IT ALL.
ME TOO.
I'D WAGER WE CAN BOTH AGREE ON THE PRIME SUSPECT.
IT'S GOTTA BE--
THE ROGUE!!

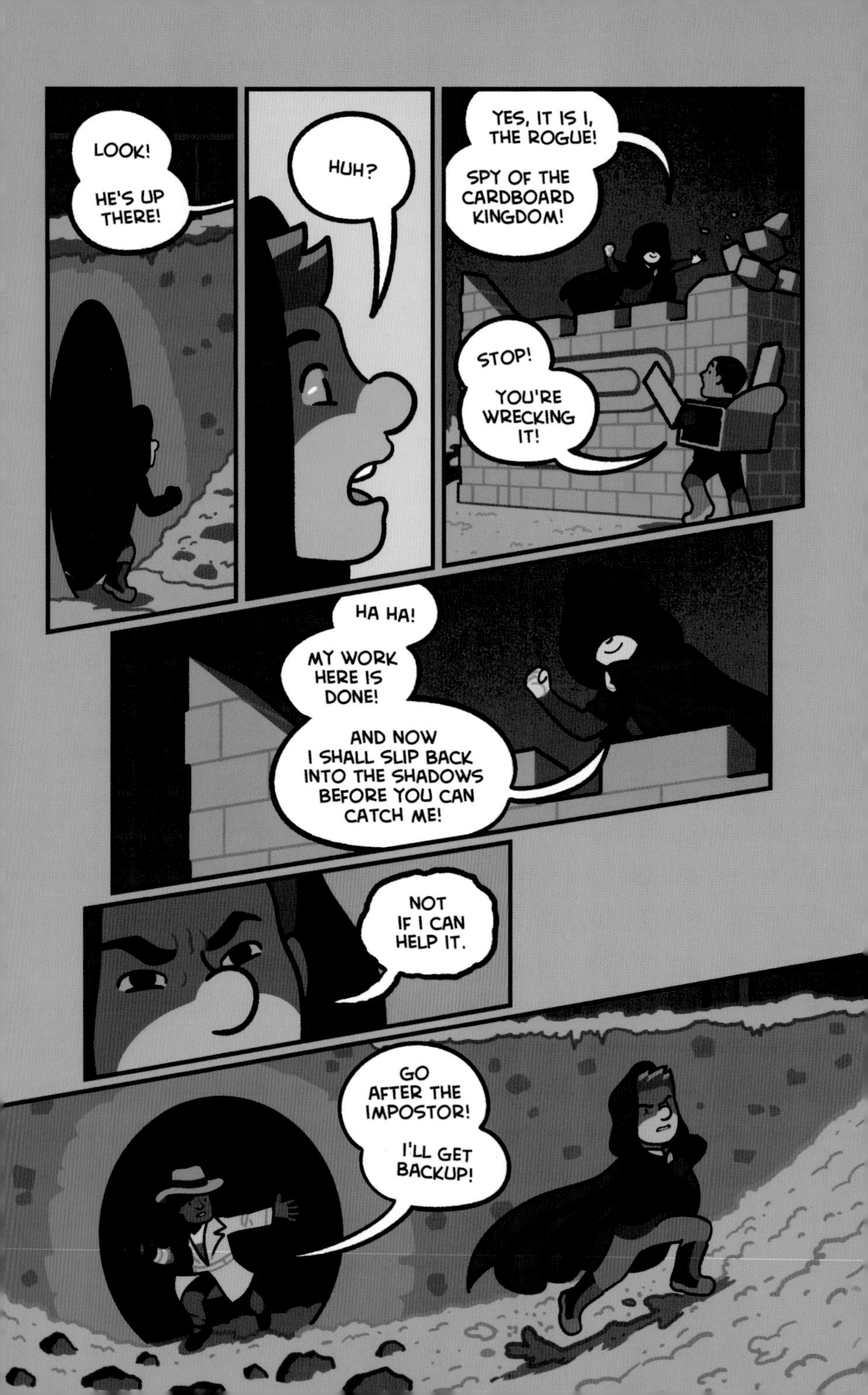
LOOK!
HE'S UP THERE!
HUH?
YES, IT IS I, THE ROGUE!
SPY OF THE CARDBOARD KINGDOM!
STOP!
YOU'RE WRECKING IT!
HA HA!
MY WORK HERE IS DONE!
AND NOW I SHALL SLIP BACK INTO THE SHADOWS BEFORE YOU CAN CATCH ME!
NOT IF I CAN HELP IT.
GO AFTER THE IMPOSTOR!
I'LL GET BACKUP!

AH HA!
A SECRET LAIR!
I'VE GOT YOU NOW!

MASTER PLAN
SMASH STUPID SNOW STUFF
USE ROBOT COSTUME TO ATTACK DRONE
GET EVERYONE ON YOUR SIDE AGAINST THE CARDBOARD KINGDOM
USE ROGUE COSTUME TO DAMAGE ICE PALACE
START AN EPIC BATTLE WITH THE CARDBOARD KINGDOM
WIN IT
HAVE A BIG PARTY WITH ALL YOUR NEW FRIENDS
THE **COPYCAT!**
YOU'VE BEEN BEHIND **EVERYTHING,** HAVEN'T YOU?!

AH!
THE SPY HIMSELF!
HAVE YOU COME TO PLAY?
PLAY?
NO, THIS ISN'T A GAME.
ISN'T IT?
IT'S BEEN FUN PLAYING YOU.
THE HOOD IS VERY DRAMATIC.

COULD YOU TAKE THAT OFF?
IT'S CREEPY.
WHY IS IT CREEPY?
IT'S YOUR COSTUME!
IT'S JUST WEIRD SEEING YOU DRESSED LIKE ME.
IT'S...
IT'S LIKE...
LIKE LOOKING IN A MIRROR?
AND WHY WOULD THAT BOTHER YOU?
I DON'T UNDERSTAND WHY YOU'VE BEEN DOING ALL OF THIS!
ALL THE SNEAKING AND THE SCHEMING...
COPYING US AND SETTING US UP!
WHAT DO YOU WANT?!
DO YOU WANT TO BE US?!
I...
I DID.

WAS IT REALLY JUST LAST WEEK?
WHEN WE SAW ALL OF YOU PLAYING IN THE PARK?
YOU HAD ALL YOUR COSTUMES AND CHARACTERS FIGURED OUT.
IT JUST...
IT LOOKED LIKE YOU WERE HAVING SO MUCH FUN TOGETHER.
WE USUALLY DO.
WE THOUGHT MAYBE WE COULD GET THE OTHER KIDS IN PARKSIDE TO PLAY LIKE THAT.
BUT THEY COULDN'T COME UP WITH THEIR CHARACTERS...
THEY DIDN'T WANT TO MAKE THEIR OWN COSTUMES...
IT JUST WASN'T WORKING.
SO THAT'S WHY YOU WANTED TO COME PLAY WITH US?
AND YOU KNOW HOW THAT TURNED OUT.

LOOK...
I'M NOT GREAT AT MAKING FRIENDS.
I...HAVE A HARD TIME **FITTING IN**.
I CAN'T IMAGINE **WHY**.
BUT I'VE LEARNED THAT SOMETIMES...
IF I LOOK AT WHAT EVERYONE ELSE IS DOING...
AND JUST COPY THAT...
I CAN TRICK THEM INTO THINKING THAT I **BELONG**.
WAIT...
ALL OF THIS WAS SO WE'D **PLAY** WITH YOU?
YOU DON'T REALLY HAVE A **CHOICE**, DO YOU?
AND NOW PARKSIDE IS PLAYING, TOO.
BUT...
YOU SMASHED OUR SNOW SCULPTURES!
YOU FRAMED **CONNIE**!
AND YOU DAMAGED...
VALKYRIE?!
YEAH? SO? WHAT'S THE **BIG DEAL**?
Use ROGUE COSTUME TO DAMAGE ICE PALACE
VMMMMM

YOUR "MASTER PLAN" HAS BROUGHT OUR TWO KINGDOMS TO THE BRINK OF ALL-OUT BATTLE!
EXACTLY!
I WORKED HARD FOR THAT.
AND I'M GOING TO WIN.
YOU WANT TO WIN?!
WHAT'S THE POINT OF PLAYING IF YOU DON'T?
WHAT DO YOU THINK WINNING EVEN MEANS?
IT MEANS--
IT MEANS YOU WERE WRONG!!
ALL OF YOU!
WE ARE GOOD ENOUGH TO PLAY WITH YOU!
WE'RE JUST AS GOOD!
BETTER!!

I TOLD YOU, 'CAT. THIS ISN'T A GAME.
NOT ONE THAT ANY OF US CAN WIN.
I CAN.
I WILL.
OH YEAH?
WILL YOUR FRIENDS STILL FIGHT AT YOUR SIDE WHEN THEY SEE THIS?
HEY!
LOOK! OVER THERE!
WHA-- VALKYRIE!!
VMMMMMM

YOU STINKY LITTLE SPY!!
ARE-- ARE YOU RECORDING?
TRINI!
ISABELA!!
SHE CONFESSED! EVERYTHING!
ON CAMERA!
UM, ABOUT THAT...
WE'VE GOTTA GO!
RIGHT, RIGHT!!
VMMMMMMMMM

WRITTEN AND ILLUSTRATED BY CHAD SELL

THE NEXT DAY...
the SORCERY SHOWDOWN
THE FINAL BATTLE
of
THE CARDBOARD KINGDOM
vs
PARKSIDE
TODAY AT THE PARK
the SORCERY SHOWDOWN
THE FINAL BATTLE

DO YOU HAVE IT?
HUH? WHAT?
THE COPYCAT'S CONFESSION!
YOU GOT IT ALL ON VIDEO, RIGHT?
I TRIED TO TELL YOU... VALKYRIE'S CAMERA IS JUST TO SEE WHERE SHE'S GOING!
WHAT?
IT DOESN'T RECORD ANYTHING! THERE'S NO VIDEO!
YOU MEAN...
I GOT THE MASTERMIND BEHIND THIS WHOLE MESS TO CONFESS EVERYTHING...
AND WE'RE NOT ANY CLOSER TO STOPPING HER SCHEME?

THAT'S NOT THE CASE, ACTUALLY.
THE COPYCAT PROBABLY THINKS VALKYRIE RECORDED THE WHOLE THING, JUST LIKE WE DID.
AH HA! SO WE'LL BLUFF!
HUH?
WE CAN TELL THE COPYCAT WE'VE GOT HER WHOLE CONFESSION ON TAPE...
AND MAYBE SHE'LL BACK DOWN.
BUT... BUT THAT WOULD BE LYING.
SO?
WE ARE SCIENTISTS AND SCHOLARS, SIR! WE WILL DECEIVE NO ONE!
BUT A BATTLE COULD BREAK OUT AT ANY MOMENT!
KIDS COULD GET HURT!

THE SCIENCE SQUAD STANDS **TOGETHER** ON THIS.
BUT...
YOU...
IT'S HOPELESS, ROGUE.
THEY WON'T DO IT.
ALL IS NOT LOST! WE'VE GATHERED SO MUCH **EVIDENCE**!
IF WE COULD JUST PIECE IT ALL TOGETHER IN A COMPELLING CASE, WE COULD STOP THE COPYCAT IN HER TRACKS!
HOW?
BY STEALING HER **BOOTS**?
OR...?
WAIT.
WOULD PART OF HER **MASTER PLAN** HELP WITH THAT?

INCREDIBLE!
SO THAT'S WHAT SHE WAS PLANNING!
THIS IS PRECISELY WHAT WE NEEDED!
YEAH!
SO, DO YOU THINK WE CRACKED THE CASE?
WELL...
WE MADE A GOOD TEAM, BUT...
BUT IT MIGHT BE TOO LATE, RIGHT?
RIGHT.

THIS "SHOWDOWN" IS HAPPENING TODAY AT THE PARK.
WE DON'T HAVE MUCH TIME.
the SORCERY SHOWDOWN
THE FINAL BATTLE OF THE CARDBOARD KINGDOM VS. PARKSIDE
TODAY AT THE PARK
YEAH, I DON'T KNOW WHAT JACK'S PLANNING...
I'M WORRIED THE OTHER KIDS WON'T LISTEN TO US.
THEY MIGHT NOT WANT TO HEAR THE TRUTH.
WHAT IF THEY WOULD RATHER JUST FIGHT?
I'LL HEAD TO THE PARK AND SEE WHAT I CAN DO.
SOUNDS GOOD.
I'LL MEET YOU THERE WITH THE SCIENCE SQUAD WHEN WE'RE READY.
GOOD LUCK, INVESTIGATOR!
WE'RE ALL GOING TO NEED IT!

the SORCERY SHOWDOWN
THE FINAL BATTLE
OF
THE CARDBOARD KINGDOM
VS.
PARKSIDE
TODAY
AT THE
PARK

OKAY...
IT LOOKS LIKE I'VE GOT EVERYTHING.
NOW, WHERE'S...?
NANDO! THERE YOU ARE! WE NEED TO GET SET UP!
EVERYONE WILL BE HERE SOON!
I KNOW, I-- JUST GIVE ME A SEC.
ARE YOU OKAY?
ARE YOU NERVOUS?
ONLY A **LITTLE**.
WELL, **I'M** NERVOUS.
CAN... CAN WE REALLY PULL THIS OFF?
IT'LL BE THE SHOWDOWN OF THE CENTURY!

JACK!
WHAT'S GOING ON?
LOOK, THEY'RE HERE!
NECROMANCER!
THE SKELETON CREW IS READY TO FIGHT!
IN THE FINAL BATTLE BETWEEN PARKSIDE AND THE CARDBOARD KINGDOM!!
HUH?
NO, NO, THAT'S NOT--
THE BATTLE IS BETWEEN THE SORCERESS AND ME. WE'VE GOT IT ALL PLANNED OUT.
TAKE YOUR SEATS. WE'LL BE STARTING SOON.
THE SHOWDOWN IS BETWEEN THE TWO OF YOU?
YOU WANT THE REST OF US TO JUST WATCH?
WE WANT TO SHOW YOU WHAT RIVALS CAN ACCOMPLISH... TOGETHER?
HMPH!

HEY!
YOU'RE SUPPOSED TO STAY ON YOUR SIDE OF THE BRIDGE!
WE'LL JUST BE A MINUTE!
SORRY!
LET'S GO, BECKY!
HEY, JACK?
HOW IS YOUR MAGIC SHOW GOING TO BE THE "FINAL BATTLE" BETWEEN OUR KINGDOMS?
NO SPOILERS, BUT...
WE'RE GOING TO SHOW YOU THE MAGIC...OF FRIENDSHIP.
OR... RIVALS.
FRENEMIES. WHATEVER.
NATE, WE NEED TO TALK TO THE COPYCAT BEFORE IT'S TOO LATE!
WE CAN STILL STOP THIS BEFORE IT GETS UGLY.
OKAY, LET'S GO!
AND THEN YOU CAN TRY YOUR LITTLE SHOW, JACK.
HURRY UP! WE'RE NOT STARTING LATE!

SO, WAIT...
WHAT'S THE PLAN?
DON'T YOU SEE?
JACK'S GATHERED ALL THE PARKSIDE KIDS IN ONE PLACE--
IT'S THE PERFECT OPPORTUNITY FOR A SUPER-SECRET SNEAK ATTACK!
BUT... DOES JACK KNOW THAT?
NO, THAT'S THE SUPER-SECRET PART!
THIS IS LOGICAL.
JUST WAIT FOR MY SIGNAL...
AND THEN OUR STINKY SLIMEBALLS WILL RAIN DOWN ON ALL OUR ENEMIES!
MWAHAHAHA!!!!

HEY, MR. MONEYBAGS! I'VE GOT A BUSINESS PROPOSAL FOR YOU!
NO, SORRY, I DON'T WANT ANY COCOA, THANKS.
WE'RE NOT--
I--
DEEP BREATHS, ALICE.
WE KNOW WHERE YOU GET THOSE FANCY CANDY BARS.
I-- SO?
WE MET YOUR DAD, TOO. GREAT GUY.
I CAN'T IMAGINE HOW HE'D FEEL FINDING OUT HIS SON MIKHAIL WAS STEALING FROM HIS OWN STORE.
ARE...
ARE YOU TRYING TO BLACKMAIL ME?
NO, I-- I WANT TO FIND A WAY TO WORK TOGETHER INSTEAD OF--
I GET IT.
YOU SEE MY MERCENARY MECH SQUAD HERE...
THEIR POWER ARMOR AND INVINCIBLE FORCE FIELDS...
AND YOU'VE COME TO BEG FOR MERCY BEFORE WE CRUSH YOUR KINGDOM.
THAT'S--
YOU--
I'M GONNA--
DEEEEEP BREATHS, ALICE.

MIGUEL TOLD ME EVERYTHING, COPYCAT!
WE'RE GIVING YOU ONE LAST CHANCE TO CALL THIS OFF BEFORE--
CALL IT OFF?
WHY WOULD WE DO THAT?
MY KITTY CLONES CAN COPY ANYTHING YOU CAN DO.
WE'RE UNSTOPPABLE.
WILL THEY STILL PLAY ALONG IF THEY KNOW YOU'VE BEEN PULLING THEIR PUPPET STRINGS?
THAT YOU'VE FOOLED EVERYONE IN PARKSIDE?
THEY WON'T BELIEVE YOU!
WE'VE GOT EVIDENCE!
OUR SCIENCE SQUAD IS PUTTING IT TOGETHER, AND--
YAWWWN!
WHO WANTS TO LISTEN TO THEIR LECTURES?
AND...
AND WE HAVE IT ALL ON VIDEO.
YOUR WHOLE CONFESSION.
YOU DO?
OR... DO YOU?
I...
IT DOESN'T MATTER!
IT'S TOO LATE!
IT'S TOO LATE FOR ALL OF YOU!

ATTENTION, EVERYONE!!
TAKE YOUR SEATS ON **YOUR OWN** SIDES OF THE BRIDGE! THANK YOU!
WE'RE READY TO START THE SHOWDOWN!
PLEASE TURN OFF YOUR PHONES!!
AND NO FILMING DURING THE PERFORMANCE.
THERE WILL **NOT** BE AN INTERMISSION...
BUT THERE WILL BE SNACKS AFTERWARD AT THE DRAGON'S HEAD INN.
NANDO, START THE MUSIC!
WHICH BUTTON IS IT?
THIS ONE?
NO, LOOK...
IT'S RIGHT--
NOW!!!

WHAT?!
SAM, NO!!
NANDO!
GET OUT
OF THE
WAY!!
WHA--
PLK
SPLT
SPLSH
PFFT
COUGH!

WAS THIS YOUR WHOLE PLAN?
TO TRICK ME INTO THINKING WE WERE FRIENDS?!
NO!
ARE YOU OKAY?!
THAT'S...
THAT'S JAM, RIGHT?
WE'VE BEEN BETRAYED!
SKELETON CREW, ATTACK!!!
WHOOO!!!
NO! I--
MERCENARY MECH SQUAD, LET'S MARCH!
$
GET THEM ALL, KITTY CLONES!
TODAY, WE CRUSH THE CARDBOARD KINGDOM!

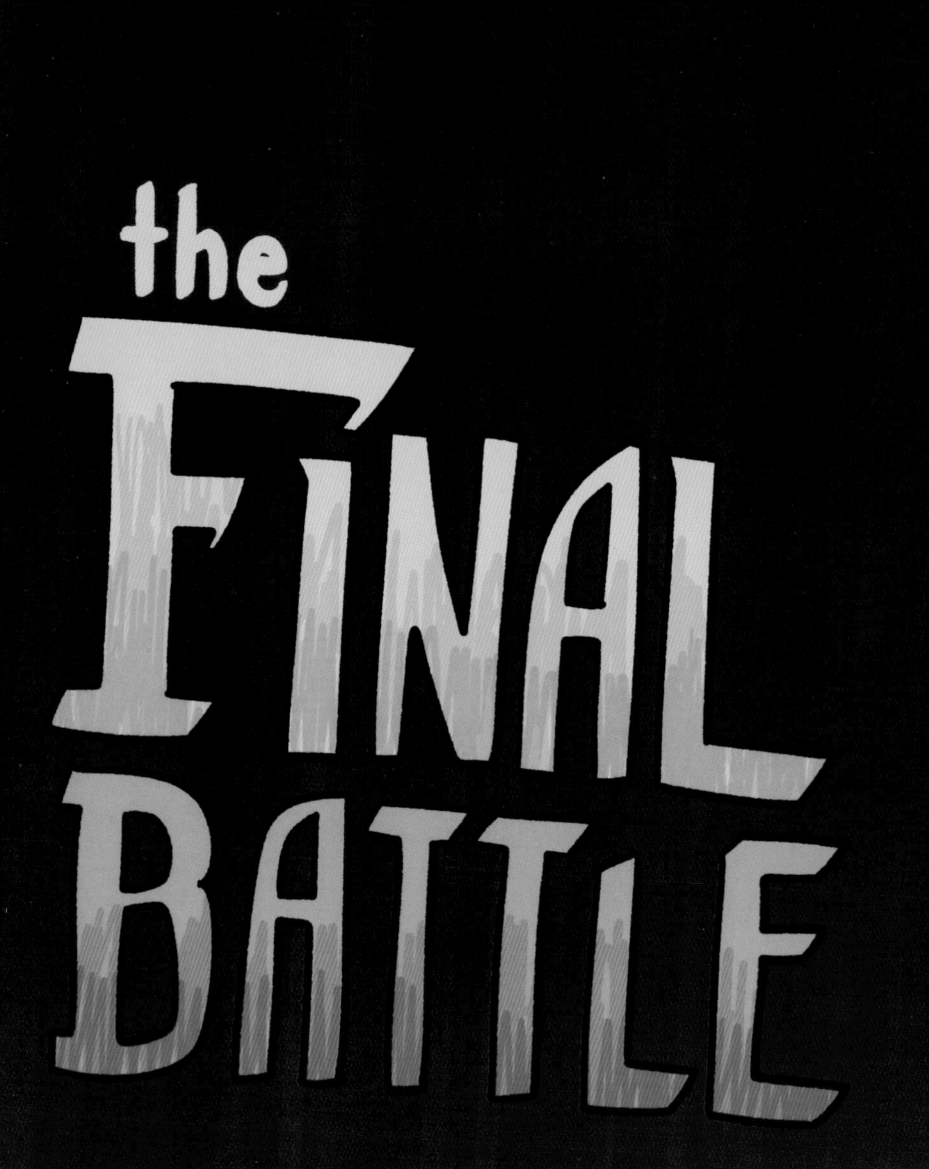

WRITTEN AND ILLUSTRATED BY CHAD SELL

GET BACK!
OR...
OR I'LL SHATTER YOU ALL!
I CAN PUT THEM BACK TOGETHER FASTER THAN YOU CAN BLAST THEM!
ARISE, MY WARRIOR!
DESTROY THIS TREACHEROUS WITCH!
AHHH!!!
NO, DON'T TOUCH ME WITH YOUR GROSS, POKEY BONES!
EWWWW!!!

EWWW! IT STINKS!!
YUCK!!
WE'VE GOT YOU, JACK!
THESE SLIMEBALLS WILL KEEP 'EM STINKY FOR DAYS!
I KNOW! I'M COVERED IN THEM!
YOU RUINED EVERYTHING!
THE NECROMANCER THINKS THAT I TRICKED HER!
BUT--
WASN'T THAT THE WHOLE POINT?!
TO TRICK HER WITH OUR SUPER-SECRET SNEAK ATTACK?!

MY BONE DAGGERS WILL STAB YOU BOTH IN THE BACK...
JUST LIKE YOU DID TO ME!!
NOOOO!!!
AAGGHH!
THIS-- THIS ISN'T HOW THE SHOWDOWN WAS SUPPOSED TO END.
WHAT DO YOU MEAN?
WE... WERE BOTH GOING TO WIN.
ONWARD, WARRIORS!
BOTH OF YOU?! I THOUGHT YOU HATED THE NECROMANCER!
I DO!
BUT I DON'T!
BUT I DO!
I...DON'T KNOW.
HUMANS ARE SO CONFUSING.

YOU WON'T GET PAST US, MR. MILLIONAIRE!
OH, JUST TRY AND STOP ME!
SORRY, GIRLS.
THESE FORCE FIELDS ARE THE BEST MONEY CAN BUY!
NOTHING GETS PAST THEM!

WE'LL SEE ABOUT THAT, WON'T WE, PETER?
OH, HELLO AGAIN!
WELL, THAT WAS A GOOD TRY.
BUT LET'S SKIP TO THE END, OKAY?
WE WIN, YOU LOSE.

KEEP IT MOVING, MECHS!
TIME IS MONEY!
BUT--
WE'RE NOT DONE!
YES, WE ARE!
IS THIS REALLY HOW YOU PARKSIDE KIDS WANT TO PLAY?
WHAT DO YOU MEAN?
HIM ORDERING YOU AROUND LIKE THAT?
SHE'S JUST BEING A SORE LOSER!
LET'S GO!
BUT...SHE AND I ARE TALKING!
SHE CAN'T TALK IF SHE'S ZAPPED WITH A BAZILLION VOLTS OF ELECTRICITY!
YOU CAN'T JUST--
BZZZT!!

THINGS AREN'T LOOKING SO GOOD FOR YOUR CUTE LITTLE KINGDOM, ARE THEY?
WE'VE GOT TO STOP THE BATTLE!
OUR EVIDENCE IS READY!
WE JUST NEED A **CHANCE**!
I THINK IT'S A LITTLE TOO **LATE** FOR THAT!
BUT... BUT MAYBE NOT!
WHAT ARE YOU GOING TO **DO**, ROGUE?
ALL YOUR FRIENDS HAVE FALLEN.
IT'S JUST YOU AND YOUR PRECIOUS PRINCE AGAINST ME AND MY KITTY CLONES!

LOOK, I--I...
WHEN YOU COPIED ME, IT DID CREEP ME OUT.
RARRGH!!
BUT THAT'S MY OWN FAULT!
MY OWN ISSUE!
I DIDN'T LIKE SEEING HOW EVERYONE ELSE SEES ME!
IT'S NOT EASY LOOKING IN THE MIRROR AND ADMITTING YOU MESSED UP.
BUT I CAN. I WILL.
LIKE YOUR PRINCE SAID...
IT'S A LITTLE LATE FOR THAT!
I'M SORRY, COPYCAT.
I MISUNDERSTOOD YOU FROM THE START.

YOU JUST WANTED TO BELONG...
TO HAVE A PLACE IN THE CARDBOARD KINGDOM.
I SHOULD HAVE SEEN THAT MORE CLEARLY.
I SHOULD HAVE SEEN YOU MORE CLEARLY.
WILL YOU JUST SHUT UP AND FIGHT ME?!
NO.
NOT ANYMORE.

RARRGHH!!!
MIGUEL!!
HOW ADORABLE!
THE PERFECT LITTLE PRINCE WANTS TO SAVE THE DAY!
YOU'RE WRONG, COPYCAT...
I'VE STOPPED TRYING TO BE PERFECT.

AAH!
BUT I WILL DO EVERYTHING I CAN TO SAVE OUR KINGDOM!
NECROMANCER!
MILLIONAIRE!
HELP!!
DO THEY KNOW, COPYCAT?
HOW YOU USED THEM AS PART OF YOUR MASTER PLAN?
DON'T LISTEN TO THEM!
ATTACK!!!
NO! LISTEN!
LET US MAKE OUR CASE!

WHAT DID THEY SAY?
SOMETHING ABOUT... A MASTER PLAN?
VMMMMMMMM
I SAID DON'T LISTEN TO THEM! WE'VE ALMOST--
HEY!! NO FAIR! GIVE IT BACK!
NOT UNTIL YOU STOP AND HEAR THE TRUTH!
SCIENCE SQUAD, PRESENT THE EVIDENCE!!

YOU WANT US TO READ ALL THAT?
WHAT IS IT?
THE COPYCAT CONSPIRACY
IT'S PROOF!
THAT ALL OUR FIGHTING IS PART OF THE COPYCAT'S PLAN!
TO SCARE YOU INTO THINKING WE WERE YOUR ENEMY!
TO TURN ALL OF PARKSIDE AGAINST US!
DON'T FALL FOR IT!
WE'VE ALMOST WON!
THIS IS JUST A DESPERATE LAST-MINUTE TRICK!!
YOU'RE THE ONLY TRICKSTER HERE, COPYCAT!
YOU DAMAGED OUR SNOW SCULPTURES!
YOU ATTACKED VALKYRIE!
THE PROOF'S RIGHT HERE!
THE COPYCAT CONSPIRACY

ALL OF THIS?
IT WAS YOUR FAULT?
NOT... ENTIRELY.
WHAT DO YOU MEAN?
WHEN WE FIRST MET...
I DID FEEL THREATENED BY YOU.
LIKE...
THERE COULDN'T POSSIBLY BE TWO MAGICAL BOYS LIKE US IN THE WORLD.
BUT...
I WAS WRONG.
YOU DIDN'T MAKE ME ANY LESS MAGICAL.
YOU MADE ME MORE.
AND...I WAS REALLY EXCITED ABOUT OUR SHOWDOWN.
I...
ME TOO, JACK.

SO THIS WAS JUST A GAME?
THAT WE'VE ALL JUST LOST?
NOT NECESSARILY!
WHAT ARE YOU PROPOSING?
LOOK, WE DIDN'T GET OFF TO A GREAT START.
AND MAYBE THAT WAS PARTLY MY FAULT.
MAYBE?
BUT I WASN'T TRYING TO BLACKMAIL YOU ABOUT THE CANDY YOU STOLE FROM YOUR PARENTS' STORE.
I--I WANTED TO HELP YOU PAY THEM BACK FOR IT.
WHAT?!
YOU EXPECT ME TO JUST... TAKE YOUR MONEY?
OF COURSE NOT!!
I THINK... I THINK MAYBE WE COULD GO INTO BUSINESS TOGETHER.
OH.
WELL... HUH.
THAT'S VERY INTERESTING.

THIS ISN'T HOW IT ENDS! NOT FOR ME!!
I DON'T NEED ANY OF YOU!
I'M NOT LOSING THIS BATTLE!
NO ONE HAS TO LOSE, COPYCAT.
NOT IF WE FIGURE OUT HOW TO BUILD A BETTER KINGDOM TOGETHER.
WHAT...
WHAT ARE YOU SAYING?
THIS MIGHT SOUND CORNY...
BUT I MEAN IT.
I THINK THERE'S ROOM FOR EVERYONE IN THIS KINGDOM, COPYCAT.
IF YOU'D STILL LIKE A PLACE IN IT.

YOU--
BUT--
ARE YOU **SERIOUS**?
I AM.
SO, HERE, COPYCAT...
COPY ME.
LET'S BRING THIS TO AN END.
IN THE HOPE OF A NEW BEGINNING.

THE COPYCAT CONSPIRACY

OKAY!
FINE!!!
YOU WIN!!
KRNCH
NO, COPYCAT!
WE'VE ALL WON!
LET'S PARTY!
HURRAY!!!!
WHOOOO!!!!

HEY.
I WAS THINKING...
HUH?
I FEEL LIKE THE TWO SNEAKIEST KIDS IN THE KINGDOM SHOULD STICK TOGETHER.
HOW DOES THAT SOUND?
HMPH.
I'M **WAY** SNEAKIER.
REALLY? DID YOU KNOW I WAS **BLUFFING**?
ABOUT VALKYRIE'S VIDEO?
DANG.
SNEAKY.

a new beginning

WRITTEN BY VID ALLIGER AND CHAD SELL
ILLUSTRATED BY CHAD SELL

THE NEXT DAY...
AT THE UNVEILING OF ELIJAH'S NEW PROJECT IN THE PARK...
WOW, ELIJAH...
IT'S HUGE!
BUT... WHAT IS IT?
WELL, OBVIOUSLY, IT'S...UH...
ACTUALLY, ELIJAH, YOU'RE THE ARTIST.
WHY DON'T YOU TELL US WHAT IT IS?
IT'S... A MONUMENT.

IT'S NOT SUPPOSED TO BE ANY ONE THING.
BUT I HOPE THAT WHEN PEOPLE LOOK AT IT...
THEY THINK OF PEACE.
PEACE BETWEEN KINGDOMS.
PEACE BETWEEN NEIGHBORHOODS.
NOW AND FOREVER.
OR...
AT LEAST... UNTIL IT MELTS.

SO...
WHAT DO YOU THINK?
IT'S BETTER THAN THE ZOMBIE REINDEER.
NO, ABOUT **PEACE**!
BETWEEN OUR KINGDOMS!
BETWEEN...US?
WELL...
AFTER ALL OUR BATTLES AND BETRAYALS...
DOESN'T **PEACE** SOUND A LITTLE... **BORING**?
THERE'S **PLENTY** TO DO IN PEACETIME!
DARK ALLIANCES, SINISTER SCHEMES...
MAYBE YOU CAN EVEN TEACH ME HOW TO DO THAT COOL EYE MAKEUP!
THAT IS...
IF YOU THINK I CAN PULL IT OFF.
LET'S MARK **THAT** AS A "MAYBE."

WE'RE READY!
SO GET UP HERE BEFORE IT GETS COLD!
FREE COCOA!
COURTESY OF THE DRAGON'S HEAD INN
BEFORE WHAT GETS COLD?
TO CELEBRATE OUR NEW ALLIANCE, WE'RE GIVING OUT FREE COCOA!
TO KIDS FROM BOTH KINGDOMS!
BUT JUST PLAIN COCOA, NOT PEPPERMINT OR ANY OF THE FANCY STUFF!
ONE CUP PER KID!
AND NO FREE REFILLS!
GET IN LINE!
THERE'S PLENTY FOR EVERYBODY!
HMM...

YOU'RE JUST GIVING AWAY YOUR PRODUCT? FOR FREE?
WHAT KIND OF BUSINESS IS THAT?
GEEZ, MIKHAIL! LEARN SOME PEOPLE SKILLS!
WE'RE BUILDING BRAND AWARENESS!
KIDS FROM BOTH KINGDOMS CAN SEE THAT THEIR LOCAL DRAGON'S HEAD INN HAS EVERYTHING THEY NEED!
BUT-- BUT PARKSIDE DOESN'T HAVE A DRAGON'S HEAD INN.
NOT YET!
BUT...WHAT IF YOU STARTED ONE?
YOU WANT ME TO WORK FOR YOU?!
WE'RE OFFERING YOU AN EXCLUSIVE FRANCHISING OPPORTUNITY.
PARKSIDE'S DRAGON'S HEAD INN WOULD BE ALL YOURS.
WE CAN NEGOTIATE TERMS LATER.
HMM.
DEAL.

WHY MUST WE WAIT IN LINE WITH THE PUNY HUMANS?
I THOUGHT WE WERE GOING TO **OVERTHROW** THE HUMANS!
HAVE PATIENCE. THE ROBOT REVOLUTION IS **INEVITABLE.**
WHEN'S... **INEDIBLE**?
IS IT BEFORE WE **LEAVE** TOMORROW?
TOMORROW? HAS IT BEEN A WEEK ALREADY?
WE DON'T WANNA GO!
THIS WAS THE BEST TRIP EVER!
DO YOU THINK WE CAN COME BACK IN THE SPRING?
CAN WE WAIT TO OVERTHROW HUMANITY **THEN**?
AFFIRMATIVE.

ALICE AND BECKY HAVE THE BEST COCOA!
JUST WAIT!
COOL!
BUT...
HOW WILL I DRINK IT?
UH...
WITH YOUR MOUTH?
NO, I MEAN...
HOW WILL I HOLD IT WITH THESE ON?
DON'T WORRY, I'M THE MASTER OF MONSTER HANDS!
I'LL TEACH YOU MY TRICKS IN NO TIME!
HAHAHAHA!!
SURE, THE SNOW FORT IS COOL, BUT...
WE CAN MAKE AN EVEN BIGGER PILLOW FORT TONIGHT AT OUR SLEEPOVER!
RIGHT, PETE?
CAN YOU BRING EXTRA BLANKETS?
AND EVERY PILLOW YOU'VE GOT!
SOUND GOOD?

THIS IS NICE, RIGHT?
IT'S STILL TOO HOT FOR ME.
NO, I MEANT... ALL THIS.
SEEING EVERYBODY HERE, JUST TALKING, HAVING COCOA TOGETHER.
BUT IT'S NOT EVERYBODY, NATE.
WHERE'S THE COPYCAT?
WHY DIDN'T SHE COME?
I REALLY THOUGHT...
I HOPED THAT MAYBE...
SHE WOULD...
BOO!!!
AAHHH!!!

HAHAHA!
COPYCAT!!
I SPILLED MY COCOA!
I KNOW!
I TOTALLY GOT YOU.
HEH HEH!
OKAY, YEAH, YOU DID.
SNEAKY.
I WASN'T SURE IF YOU'D SHOW UP.
ME NEITHER.
BUT... I'M GLAD YOU DID.
ME TOO.

HERE'S SOMETHING I CAN'T FIGURE OUT...
WHY STILL WEAR THOSE COSTUMES?
BECAUSE... THEY'RE COOL?
YEAH, I LIKE ALL THIS CARDBOARD STUFF.
BUT YOU DON'T WANT TO BE WHAT SOMEONE ELSE MADE YOU BE, DO YOU?
NO WAY!
WE'RE DONE WITH THAT!
SO...NOW THAT THE BATTLE IS OVER...
WHAT DO YOU WANT TO DO?
WHO DO YOU WANT TO BE?
HUH...
I'M NOT SURE...
THAT'S A LOT TO FIGURE OUT.
YEAH, IT IS.
BUT...
I HAVE SOME NEW FRIENDS WHO MIGHT BE ABLE TO HELP.

IF YOU WANT TO MAKE SOME COSTUMES OF YOUR OWN...
WE HAVE EVERYTHING YOU NEED!
WE'VE GOT TAPE, PAINT, MARKERS...
AND... CARDBOARD?
TONS!!
SO WE DON'T HAVE TO BE SKELETONS?
OR KITTY CLONES?
YOU CAN BE ANYTHING YOU CAN IMAGINE!
OOOH!
I HAVE AN IDEA!!
THEN STEP RIGHT UP!
LET'S GET STARTED!

WELCOME TO THE CARDBOARD KINGDOM!
WHAT DO YOU WANT TO BE?

THE KNIGHT'S ARMORY
LAIR OF THE SORCERESS!
THE PRINCE'S CASTLE
THE ROGUE'S DEN
SWING SET
BACKYARD OF THE BEAST
PRINCE'S POOL
THE DRAGON'S HEAD INN
THE PROFESSOR'S LIBRARY
HUNTER'S LODGE
BECKY THE BLACKSMITH
BIG BANSHEE'S BOG
ALICE THE ALCHEMIST
THE GARGOYLE'S ROOST
THE ANIMAL QUEEN'S JUNGLE
THE SCRIBE'S ARCHIVE

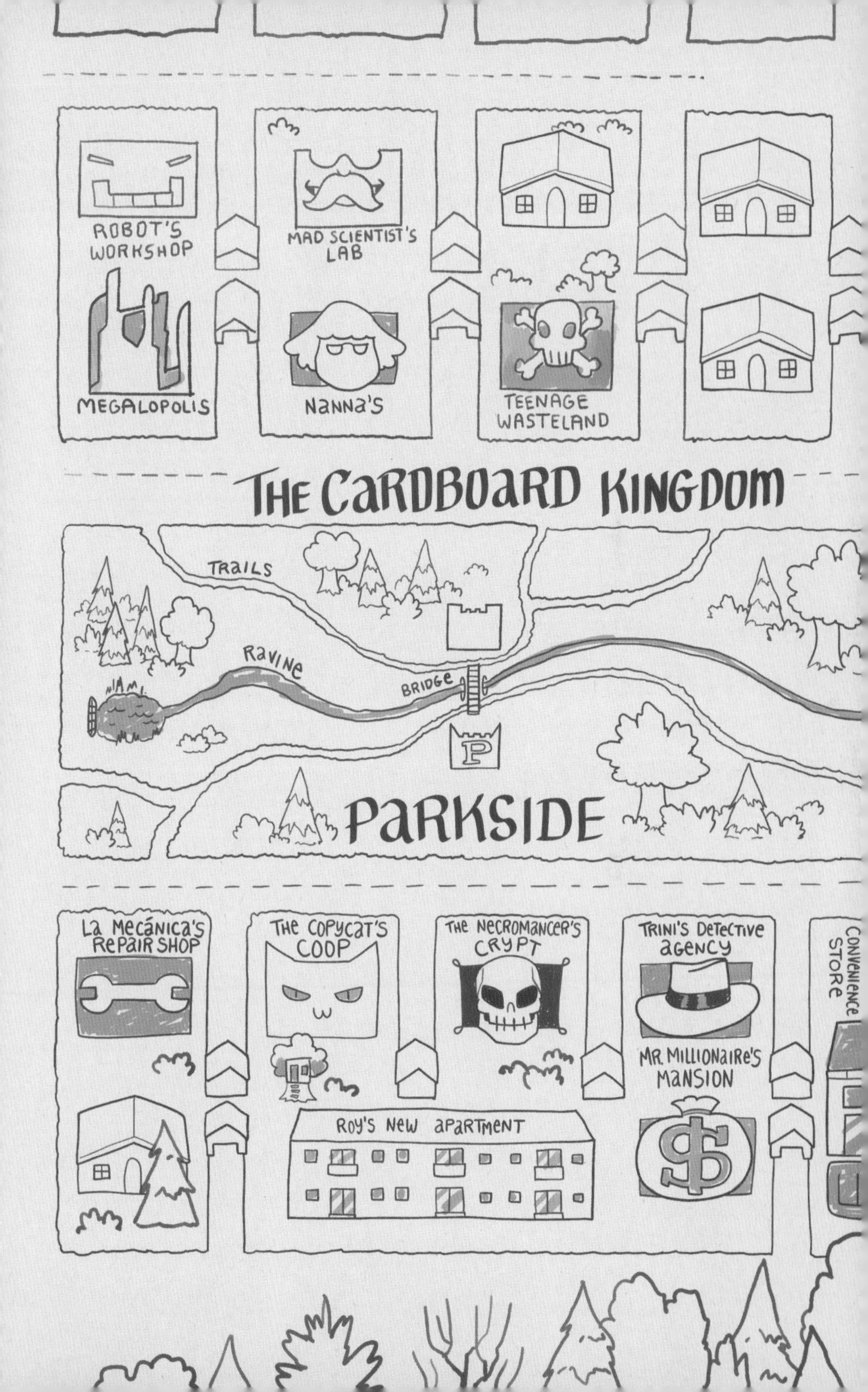
ROBOT'S WORKSHOP
MAD SCIENTIST'S LAB
MEGALOPOLIS
Nanna's
TEENAGE WASTELAND
THE CARDBOARD KINGDOM
TRAILS
Ravine
BRIDGE
P
PARKSIDE
La Mecánica's Repair Shop
The Copycat's Coop
The Necromancer's Crypt
Trini's Detective agency
Convenience Store
Mr. Millionaire's Mansion
Roy's New apartment

HOW WE BUILT THE KINGDOM

Can *anybody* join the Cardboard Kingdom? That's what Chad Sell asked himself when he first started work on *Snow and Sorcery*. The Cardboard Kingdom series has always been about kids creating an inclusive and welcoming community together. But how can the Cardboard Kingdom keep growing as it inspires kids in nearby neighborhoods to join the adventures? What kinds of clashes and conflicts will result, and how can those differences be overcome? The writers of *The Cardboard Kingdom* came up with their own answers to these questions. They have worked together in a unique collaborative process that resulted in the book you've just read. And they've also welcomed a new writer to the team: Jasmine Walls!

JAY FULLER-NG

"The Secret Weapons Lab," "Finishing the Fort"

Jay is a cartoonist living in Brooklyn, New York, with his husband, Kevin, and their little corgi, Darwin. He writes and illustrates the comic *The Boy in Pink Earmuffs*. Jay is inspired to tell the stories he lived growing up as a queer youth building fierce snow fortresses, dressing up fabulous snow people, and occasionally slaying the competition in a friendly snowball fight.

DAVID DEMEO

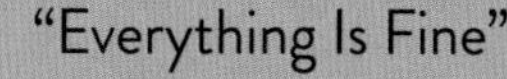

"Everything Is Fine"

David is an artist and designer for his own line of jewelry and clothing, POPabyss. It has always been his dream to become a writer, and as an original contributing author to the Cardboard Kingdom series, he realized that dream. He continues to pursue various artistic and writing projects while taking breaks for mini dance parties, *Steven Universe*, and vegan nachos. He quotes movies endlessly and does an uncanny impression of Miss Piggy. David lives in New Jersey with his fiancé, Nelson.

KATIE SCHENKEL

"Surprise Gifts and Guests," "Unleasing the Banshee"

Katie writes lots of kids' graphic novels, including *The Wolf in Unicorn's Clothing*, *My Slime Is Alive!*, and *Alice, Secret Agent of Wonderland*. She has loved getting to expand on Sophie's family and show Sophie's growth throughout the series. Katie lives in Chicago with her partner, Madison, and their three-pawed dog, Moira.

MANUEL BETANCOURT

"The Prince's Plan," "Behind Enemy Lines"

Manuel spends his days writing, baking, and watching way too many films and TV shows. He's the author of *Judy at Carnegie Hall* and *The Male Gazed*. Manuel is a firm believer in the power of stories to help us discover who we are and who we could be. It's why he's thrilled to have gone on this wintry adventure with the Prince and the Rogue, two boys who are very dear to his heart and who were inspired by his own childhood love of animated fairy tales.

VID ALLIGER

"The Undercover Android," "Vandals and Vengeance," "Payback in Parkside," "A New Beginning"

Vid is a software engineer, artist, and writer living in Houston, Texas. Like the kids in the Cardboard Kingdom, he loves expressing himself creatively, whether it's in a drawing, story, or web application. He is endlessly grateful for his incredible friends and family, and for everyone who has played a role in making the Cardboard Kingdom such a magical place, including the readers.

BARBARA PEREZ MARQUEZ

"A Break in the Storm"

Barbara is a Dominican American writer. She lives in Baltimore and has been writing since she was in seventh grade. Just like Amanda, Barbara was born and raised in the Dominican Republic, loves mustaches, and believes we can all experiment a little more in life!

JASMINE WALLS

"The Investigator"

Jasmine is a writer, artist, and editor who baked professionally and taught martial arts in her former lives. She still bakes (though she's pretty rusty at martial arts) and has a deep love for imaginary worlds and the characters who inhabit them. She lives in California with two dogs and a large stash of quality hot chocolate.

CLOUD JACOBS

Cloud is a fifth-grade teacher in Stuttgart, Arkansas. When he's not reading and writing comics, he's working his way through every Star Wars book he can get his hands on. Cloud contributed the character Professor Everything, who is based on his awkward childhood, when he would usually be reading while other kids were playing football.

KRIS MOORE

Kris contributed the characters Alice the Alchemist and Becky the Blacksmith, who both appeared in the first two books of the Cardboard Kingdom series as well. Kris passed away before the first installment was published, but his partner, Weston, has permitted us to continue Alice's and Becky's adventures. We're honored that Kris's memory lives on through the unforgettable characters he created and shared with all of us.

DELETED
YOU'RE JUST A SHY LITTLE KID HIDING UNDER A HOOD.
WELL, I SEE YOU.
I SEE RIIIIIGHT THROUGH YOU.
WHY DO YOU DO THAT?
COPY OTHER KIDS?
HUH?
EVERYONE SAYS THAT LIKE IT'S A BAD THING!
DIDN'T YOU COPY A CARTOON CHARACTER FOR YOUR COSTUME?!
YEAH, BUT...
BUT NOTHING!!!
THAT'S THE WHOLE POINT OF THE CARDBOARD KINGDOM!
TO DRESS UP AS YOUR FAVORITE CHARACTERS!!!

SCENE

These pages, set in the Copycat's hideout, were in the original draft but did not make the final cut for the book!

CHARACTER DESIGNS FOR SNOW AND SORCERY

Meet the cast! To get started on the third book in the Cardboard Kingdom series, Chad Sell created designs for characters both old and new.

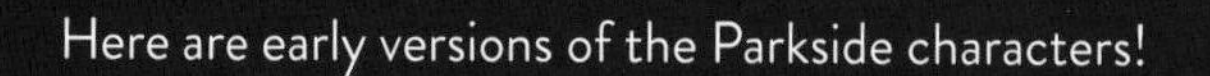
Here are early versions of the Parkside characters!

THE TRIO

THE NECROMANCER

THE COPYCAT

TRINI, THE INVESTIGATOR

ISABELA, LA MECÁNICA

THE FAMILIES OF

THE KINGDOM

CONNIE'S AUNT, UNCLE, AND COUSINS

VIV

HENRY

EDMUND AND THEODORE

REAL KIDS JOIN THE KINGDOM!

A few snapshots of the Cardboard Kingdom in the real world over the years!

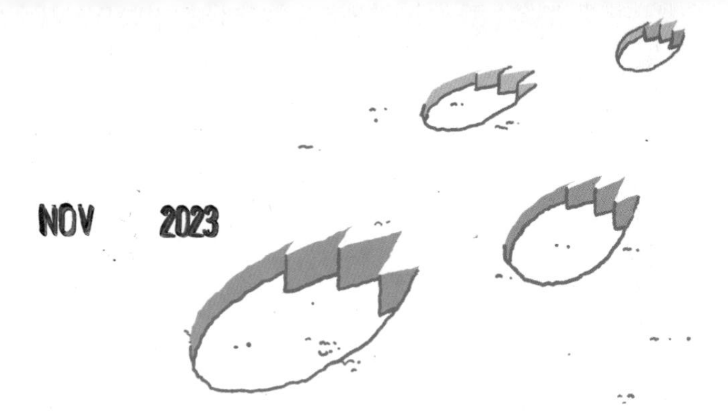

THIS IS A BORZOI BOOK PUBLISHED BY ALFRED A. KNOPF

Visit us on the Web! rhcbooks.com

Educators and librarians, for a variety of teaching tools, visit us at RHTeachersLibrarians.com

Library of Congress Cataloging-in-Publication Data is available upon request.
ISBN 978-0-593-48162-2 (trade) — ISBN 978-0-593-48163-9 (lib. bdg.) —
ISBN 978-0-593-48164-6 (ebook) — ISBN 978-0-593-48161-5 (trade pbk.)

The illustrations were created using Clip Studio Paint.
Photographs on page 311 courtesy of the author.
Book design by Juliet Goodman and Chad Sell

MANUFACTURED IN CHINA
10 9 8 7 6 5 4 3 2 1
First Edition